Turn Left for Home

Susanne Bellamy

Dedication

To the wonderful teachers and interpreters who connect those with special needs to the world.

Acknowledgements:

With thanks to my own legal eagle for explaining points of law. Any errors are mine in the pursuit of this story.

And with thanks to Annie Seaton for her editing skills and wonderful cover design.

Chapter 1

Anna Wilkins added a subtle stroke of pale green paint to her canvas and sat back from her easel. The composition of the scene was fine, but something was missing. Narrowing her eyes, she looked from the canvas to the scene beyond her easel.

Her neighbour, Rory Donovan, had moved into the frame. His bright red work shirt beside the front gates of his property, *Dawnie*, intruded on the serenity she'd been trying to capture in oils. The red was too strong for the tone of her painting, too loud, too everything. But a hint of maroon might . . .

A burst of wailing siren followed by flashing blue and red lights raced past the lower boundary fence and turned into the driveway of *Dawnie*. The police car pulled up in a swirl of dust that briefly engulfed Rory before a gust of autumn wind cleared the air.

Quickly, Anna pulled the cover over her easel. Dust motes and grit would add nothing to her painting. She dropped her paintbrush into the container of turps and picked up a thin towel serving out its final days as a work rag. An accumulation of the colours of the countryside streaked the thin material. Everything she painted lately was in country colours. Maybe that was her problem—she'd fallen into predictability as she'd bunkered down in her safe place.

Rory's red shirt moved through the scene before her, leading the police vehicle to a parking spot in the shade of a stand of three silky oak trees. As he waited, hands on hips, her gaze connected with his as she wiped her hands on the towel.

"Hey, Anna!" He beckoned her over as he walked to the fence. Behind him, Sergeant Edwards and Constable Marion

Brooks got out of the police car.

Damn, she'd hoped to disappear without being noticed. Valuing her privacy, she gave the same courtesy back to others. Only now, it was too late. God, Anna hoped he didn't assume she was snooping on him.

"Hi, Rory, what's up?" Her gaze slid past him to the police officers. Sirens and emergency lights weren't common in Lark Creek. But sirens, lights *and* side arms spelled trouble in anyone's book. Gripping the flapping halves of her painting shirt in one hand, she stopped at the fence and pressed one hand against her stomach, swallowing the bile that rose whenever there was a hint of violence.

"I've caught a thief red-handed. Got him locked in the chicken coop. Have you heard anyone around your cottage?"

Her throat closed around a cry of disbelief.

Not again.

Her stomach did a double back somersault and she pressed her hand harder against her stomach. Flicking a glance towards the cottage, her home partially hidden behind a wild mix of olive and wattle trees, she couldn't swallow the flicker of fear. The grove was a big part of what had attracted her to Cottage Farm, but now the lack of sightline threatened. Did it hide another intruder? "I've been down here painting for the past hour or two."

"You might want to check if anything's missing while the police are here."

Fearless Rory, she thought. *Easy to be so when he's young and strong.* She'd felt like that too, once upon a time. Immortal, undefeatable, ready to take on the world. Until . . .

"Will do."

Rory nodded and turned away, joining the officers and leading them up the slope towards the farmhouse.

Rory caught the thief. There's nothing to worry about. There's no one else here.

Except she didn't know if that was true.

With a caution born of bitter experience, Anna kept within the cover of the olive and wattle grove and crept towards the cottage.

Don't be a fool again. Find a weapon.

Desperately she looked around. Through the open door of the tiny wooden garden shed, a spade hung from one of two hooks. Wiping sweaty hands down her shirt, she tilted her head and held her breath.

As if that will help me to hear better.

Her tongue touched the corner of her mouth before she forced herself to move forwards, eyes darting around in search of movement. Being unaware of her surroundings and taking her personal safety for granted belonged in the past. Stepping lightly, she reached for the spade and gripped the handle with both hands before sidling along the house and peering around the corner.

The back screen door was closed, just as she'd left it. She stood to one side, pressed against the dusty, off-white wooden wall, and listened. Only the thunder of blood pounded in her ears, and the buzz of a fly landing on her nose. She scrunched her eyes closed and huffed a puff of air upwards. The fly departed and she eased the screen door open just wide enough to slip through with her spade at the ready.

Tip-toeing through the rustic kitchen, she skirted the table and paused again outside the doorway to the small lounge. Peering around the doorjamb, she checked the room with a single glance.

Still nothing.

By the time she had checked her bedroom, the second bedroom and the bathroom and found nothing, her adrenaline surge had all but gone.

Anna returned to the kitchen and dropped into one of the ladder-back chairs and leaned the spade against the table. So much for not locking doors when she was working outside. She'd allowed herself to relax and only through sheer dumb luck had she not encountered the thief this time. Well, she wasn't going to rely on luck again. From now on, every time she went beyond the herb garden, she would lock the door and—

Her gaze fell on the empty kitchen bench.

One dozen banana and blueberry mini-muffins had been cooling on the rack when she went out to paint this morning. One dozen freshly baked muffins that were now MIA. Slowly, she moved across to the bench and touched a finger to a crumb.

She wasn't imagining it—there had been a tray of muffins, and now there wasn't. Nausea welled up and she raced through the back door, pulling it closed behind her. Not another moment would she spend in the cottage until the police had been and checked it thoroughly.

She ran towards the gate that linked Cottage Farm with *Dawnie*, a relic from the days when the Donovan family had sliced a small block off the corner of their farm to make a retirement home for an earlier generation. Where were the police? What had Rory said—he'd shut the thief in the chicken coop?

Heart hammering with fear and the exertion of running up the slope, she headed past the farmhouse in the direction of the chicken coop.

Chapter 2

A cacophony of clucking and incoherent shouts drew Anna towards the Donovan's chicken coop. Mentally preparing to face the intruder who had been in her kitchen she slowed as she neared the temporary lockup. What if he was like the man who had broken into her family home and assaulted her father, knocked down her mother? What if . . .

Remembering burly arms and a tattooed neck below a face filled with malevolence, she was unprepared for the sight that greeted her. Rory stood outside the coop, fists clenched and body tensed as though he wanted nothing more than to join the fray. Two hens flapped and escaped past him, but he was intent on the action. Inside, a scrawny teenager flailed his arms. He knocked off Sergeant Edwards' hat as Constable Brooks struggled to slip handcuffs on his thin, dirty wrists.

"Uh, uh, uh." Wild animal sounds of pain, incoherent with distress and fear wrenched from the boy's throat. Sounds all too familiar in their atonal pitch.

"Stop, please." As the two officers grappled with the frightened teenager, she lunged towards the door. Rory grabbed her arm before she could enter. Constable Brooks finally managed to lock the second cuff onto the boy's wrist before taking hold of his arm.

Sergeant Edwards held the teenager's other arm and grimaced. The boy was filthy.

His body slumped in defeat as though the earth dragged him down, and his head drooped. Matted hair hid his face. Like a half-empty sack of potatoes, his knees buckled and he crumpled to the ground, held upright only by the grip of the two officers on his arms. Soundlessly, he began to rock back and forth. *Silent grief, poignant in its lack of sound . . .*

Memory slammed through Anna. The boy's body shimmered and became her father slumped on the polished wooden floor, his face distorted as blood ran freely from his head wound. Frustration, anger, helplessness bubbled through the lid she'd clamped over her emotions. Her world tilted on its axis and she slapped a hand over her mouth and groped behind her for the upright post of the doorway.

Squeezing her eyes shut she fought to stay in the here and now. Sergeant Edwards' voice, gruff with annoyance and ruffled dignity, finally broke through. Anna opened her eyes.

Marion Brooks was focused on their prisoner. When her superior officer spat out a disgruntled "Read him his rights", she began reciting the statement Anna had only ever heard on television cop shows.

"He won't understand anything you're saying." She pulled her arm free of Rory's grip. Now the boy was cuffed, Rory let her move inside the coop.

The constable stopped and looked at her with a narrow-eyed gaze at the interruption to the commission of her duty. "Do you know this person? Doesn't he speak English?"

"I have no idea if he speaks anything, but I'm pretty sure that—" She hunkered down on the concrete floor in front of the boy and touched his hand. When he glanced up she signed, *No one will hurt you. Are you okay?*

His gaze connected with hers and he tried to reply, but the handcuffs and the firm police hands holding him made signing difficult.

"What's your name?" she asked, signing, and speaking for the benefit of the police.

Kaden. At least she thought that was what he signed.

Stay calm and I'll help you. Looking up first at the

constable, then the sergeant, Anna sat back on her heels. "He's hearing-impaired. He hasn't taken in anything you've said because he hasn't seen your mouths. And he can't answer questions properly while he's wearing handcuffs."

Edwards shook his head. "No way I'm taking them off until he's in a cell. Probably on drugs and out of his mind. You saw him, spitting and scratching."

"Sergeant, he's scared and frightened, and he probably hasn't eaten for ages." She thought of her missing muffins. *Maybe they were all he'd had, which wasn't much.*

"You think he's deaf, and you can talk to him? Signing, that sort of thing?" Marion Brooks was all business, as usual. Anna liked that about her; she was calm and competent and focused on what was important.

"Yes to both questions."

The constable's gaze flicked over the boy. "Anna, would you be willing to accompany us to the station and interpret so we can take his statement and so on?"

Kaden touched her hand. His gaze had stayed on her mouth throughout the exchange with the police. *Hungry*, he signed, *thirsty. Help?*

She nodded. *The muffins weren't enough, were they?*

He shook his head and the corner of his mouth tipped up. *But good.*

She continued to both sign and speak aloud for the benefit of the police officers. "I'll come to the police station and sign for you, if you would like me to?"

Tipping his head back the boy looked at the two officers. His eyes grew wide and fear flashed through them. How old was he? He looked like he should be in school. *Help me.* As an afterthought, he added, *Please.*

"Go quietly with the police and I'll see you at the station. I'll ask them to feed you before I get there, okay?"

He nodded slowly. *Thanks.*

Hoping the promise of food might keep him calm until she got into the police station, Anna asked Constable Brooks to give the boy food and drink. "I'll get tidied up and drive down there as soon as I can." With a nod to the sergeant, she signed to Kaden, *See you soon.*

Rory stood to one side of the door, arms folded as the police led Kaden, walking between them down the slope. "Strange morning, hey?"

"And not to be repeated, I hope." Her stomach was still a tight ball of anxiety, but a thread of compassion had replaced her numbing fear.

"Had he been in your place before he came here?"

Anna nodded. "I think he was mostly after food."

"Yeah, scrawny as a rake as Mum would say. Good thing you were out painting when the police arrived." His gaze followed the group down the slope.

Marion Brooks had a hand on Kaden's head as he stepped into the back of the police vehicle. She shut the door and stepped away, lifting her cap off her head and wiping an arm across her forehead. Rory's gaze seemed fixed on the departing trio, or maybe it was Marion who held his attention, and it occurred to Anna that Rory and Marion were the same age in a town where fewer and fewer young people chose to stay.

The police car reversed out of its parking spot and headed off down the farm driveway, carrying the intruder. Anna's stomach roiled at the thought of sitting in a room with the boy who had broken into her home.

But he was so young and, if she set aside his resistance to being arrested, scared rather than violent. Telling herself this time was nothing like before didn't help much. Not when images of that other home invasion had roared back into her mind larger than life. "I'd better go. I offered to go into the station to help." Maybe a large mug of herbal tea would settle her before she had to face going into town.

As the police car turned right and disappeared up Ridge Lane, Rory turned back to her. "I never knew you could do that sign language. Pretty awesome stuff."

She tried to smile but the best she could do was nod in acknowledgement as she looked past him at the interior of the chicken coop. Shattered planks lay on the floor where the boy, or one of the police officers, had smashed into a laying house. "Looks like you've got some repairs to make."

Rory tipped his hat back on his head. Clear blue eyes twinkled in a good-looking face. "Suits me. Dad gives me all the building and repair work now. Reckons I'm a better builder than farmer."

"If you're ever looking for more work, I've got a couple of shelves need putting up."

"Consider it done."

"Thanks." Anna headed back to the cottage, stopping to collect her easel and painting gear on the way. Maybe she'd make an extra tea in her travel mug to take with her to the police station.

Chapter 3

Jack Donaldson replaced the handset in its charger, eyed the conveyance file needing immediate attention on his desk and sighed. He packed his folding keyboard and tablet into a black backpack, slung it over his shoulder and left a note telling Moira, his secretary, he'd been called to the police station. On his way out, he flipped the closed sign over before locking the door.

The joys of being a single practitioner.

Striding east along the main road through town, the scent of cinnamon wafted beneath his nose from the bakery while from the southern side of the street, stone fruits displayed in trays outside the fruiterers beckoned. They also reminded his stomach it had been a long time since breakfast.

He stopped mid-stride, turned and entered the bakery. "Hi, Darcy. I smelled your cinnamon buns from halfway down the street. Can you pop two in a bag and add them to my tab please?"

"Sure thing, Jack." With an elegant economy of movement, the red-haired baker set two buns in a shallow cardboard tray before slipping them into a brown paper packet. "Any coffee to go with that?"

"I wish. Maybe later . . . unless you've added a delivery service to your menu?" It was a joke, a wish at best, although his brain would have enjoyed the caffeine hit.

"Hmm, I'm not exactly run off my feet at the moment. Shall I make Moira one too?"

"Moira was out picking up office supplies when I left, and I'll be at the police station for the next little while, but thanks for offering."

"I can pop up to the station with it if you like. I've been

thinking about adding a delivery service to businesses in town. You could be my trial run. What do you think?"

His stomach rumbled and his brain perked up at the promise of his favourite brew. "I think you're an angel in disguise, Darcy. Thanks." He opened the door and the bell tinkled at the motion; the sound suited the angel image he'd given to Darcy.

"See you in ten." She poured beans into the grinder. The whirr of the machine cut off as the door closed behind him.

Knowing a quality coffee would be in his hand soon, Jack strode the last block to the red-brick police station, turning onto the front path as an ancient faded-green station wagon turned into the parking space marked 'Police Business Only'. The sound of squeaky brakes drew his attention to the car and the occupant. A blonde-haired woman lifted a bag from the front passenger seat and became engrossed in the contents. He walked up the steps and opened the door.

A female constable, fair hair scraped back in a tight, low bun, looked up as he approached the front counter. Figuring she must be the new constable his client, Rick Peyton, had dealt with and liked, he smiled. Her gaze assessed him and her mouth relaxed into a warm smile in return. "Good morning. Are you the lawyer?"

"Jack Donaldson, reporting in to meet with a client being held on an alleged break and enter."

"Constable Marion Brooks. We have the young man in a cell out the back for now. Would you like to meet him, although . . ." She paused and pressed her lips together. "It might be better to speak with Sergeant Edwards first."

"Any reason why I shouldn't speak to my client now?" Back in Toowoomba, he wouldn't have met with the officer in charge of the station at all, let alone before he'd spoken to his client. The change to protocol wasn't necessarily important, but he preferred everything to happen in its proper order so if there were concerns at a later date, he could demonstrate every box had been ticked.

"There's a problem; we believe he's hearing-impaired, and he hasn't spoken a word since we first apprehended him. Sometimes teenagers can be really difficult to get any information out of, and then there's now. We were lucky Rory Donovan's neighbour came over to the scene of the break in or we might not have realised so quickly that the boy wasn't able to hear us." She looked past his shoulder and her frown disappeared. "Here she is now."

Jack turned. The woman from the station wagon entered, clutching a well-worn brown leather satchel on a strap over her shoulder. She seemed to be ill-at-ease, and several times she tucked the same strand of hair behind her ears before she finally stepped up to the counter. The tip of her tongue touched the corner of her mouth.

"I'm here. Where is he?" Soft-voiced as she was, there was also a musical quality to her words that had Jack leaning closer.

He held out a hand to her. "Hi, I'm Jack Donaldson, the lawyer, and you are—"

Soft brown eyes flicked up to meet his before dropping to his hand. She eyed it for a heartbeat or two before reluctantly extending her own. A streak of blue paint marked her little finger and ran halfway across her hand before she shoved it into the pocket of her long knitted jacket. "Anna Wilkins. The police have asked me to interpret for the—for Kaden."

Marion Brooks looked at Anna and frowned. "He told you his name? What else did he say?"

Anna's shoulders hunched and she shook her head. "I *think* it may be Kaden but signing while his hands were in cuffs was awkward for him. He only told me that he was hungry and thirsty."

She seemed so out of her element and unhappy, standing in the reception area of the station, Jack felt inclined to move their conversation to a private room. "Constable Brooks, would you mind if Ms Wilkins and I continue our discussion in a private room?" Pleasant, professional, and in control of the situation—that was his aim. It worked—on the police officer, who unbolted a swinging gate and invited him through.

Anna Wilkins stood rooted to the spot. Worse, her face was pale and her hands, wrapped around the strap of her satchel, were white-knuckled.

Jack ran through their brief encounter, wondering what he might have said that had discomposed the interpreter. Nothing came to mind. Keeping his voice gentle and his expression pleasant, he gestured for her to precede him. "Ladies first."

She blinked, as though coming out of a trance, and hurried past him and into the room indicated by the constable. A subtle combination of coconut and turpentine wafted behind her. She pulled out the chair closest to the door and sat clutching the satchel on her lap.

Gently, he closed the door and took the chair facing hers. "Thank you for coming in at short notice to interpret for my client. I understand you live next door to the property where the boy— Kaden, is it—was apprehended?"

She drew in a deep breath and nodded. "I saw the police arrive and my neighbour asked me to check—to see if anyone had been in my cottage while I was down in the paddock painting." Her gaze darted away, lingering on the high window.

Putting two and two together, Jack waited until she had regained her composure before asking, "And had he been inside your home?"

"Yes." Her reply was little more than an exhalation of breath, an unwilling acknowledgement of an invasion of her home. No wonder she was tense.

"That must have been worrying. And yet you've offered to interpret for him. That's brave of you."

She pinned him with a wide-eyed gaze that suggested his comment was unwelcome with maybe a dash of stupid thrown in for good measure. "I'll be sitting here with a police officer and a lawyer, signing for a kid who's scared witless. And at the end of the interview, I'll be able to get up and walk out that door. What's brave about that?"

And that's me put in my place.

Silently applauding Anna's feisty response in the face of whatever was worrying her, Jack ploughed on. "You'll likely be facing the person who broke into your house. That takes courage, even if he turns out to be a juvenile."

She broke eye contact and opened her satchel. "It's not only the criminals you have to fear."

Negative vibes rolled off her in waves and Jack let the subject drop.

She didn't want to talk about it? Fine with him.

"Do you have your accreditation papers with you?" He would focus on his client and ensure procedure was followed . . . to the letter.

A purple folder with plastic sleeves slid across the table in his general direction. "I'm an accredited Auslan interpreter. I can do what's needed here."

He picked up the folder and leafed through it. Court work, a stint working for a government minister on policy development, numerous glowing recommendations—but no jobs listed in the past twelve months. "I'd say you're very well qualified, but why haven't you updated your resume over the past year?"

"None of your business. I can do the job, I'm currently accredited and that's all you need to know. Excuse me, I need some water." She pushed her chair back and almost ran out of the interview room, leaving Jack bewildered and vaguely annoyed.

***

Anna sagged against the water cooler, noting in a detached kind of way that her hands were shaking.

A whole year and the mere presence of a lawyer in the setting of a police station had triggered her anxiety again.

Pulling out a paper cup from the dispenser was a test of patience as her fingers fumbled, but focusing on the simple task calmed her. She pressed the button for iced water and filled her cup, slopping a little on the floor in front of the cooler when her finger was slow to lift off the lever. She drank quickly, welcoming the brain freeze, needing its numbing quality if she was going to get through this ordeal.

It's not about me this time. I can make sure Kaden gets a fair hearing.

He was unlike the thug who had broken into her family home, and certainly much younger. Vulnerable. The speed with which the boy had changed in her mind from intruder to vulnerable teenager wasn't lost on Anna. Identifying with him was a double-edged sword. He had broken into her home, violated her tenuous sanctuary and shattered her peace of mind.

Just like before. No, not him, it wasn't him before.

But despite seeing the boy in the chicken coop, fighting off the police and unable to communicate, she hadn't been able to reject his need for help, to be the bridge between the speaking world and the signed world in which the boy functioned. Setting aside her personal fears—the memories that haunted her, the nightmares from which she woke in a mess of tangled sheets—she had chosen to do what she was trained to do and help.

So suck it up, Anna, and behave like an adult, not a scared child.

Pep-talk over, she topped up her cup of water, straightened her shoulders, and returned to the interview room. "Do you have forms for me to sign, Mr Donaldson?"

He looked up from his keyboard. A lock of sandy brown hair had fallen over his forehead, and he'd slipped on a pair of reading glasses while she was out of the room. When he removed the glasses, she noticed his eyes were a warm, milk-chocolate brown and much darker than hers, which tended towards hazel in most lights. The glaring white light of the interview room would strip the warmth out of most eye colours, but his eyes caught and reflected the fluorescence like strips of radiant heat.

"Since I had no forewarning of my client's hearing impairment, I didn't know I would need such forms." He scrunched up a brown paper packet, set it inside a cardboard tray and dropped both in the rubbish bin in the corner. A hint of cinnamon hung in the air.

Anna retrieved a green folder from her satchel and took the relevant form out of the first plastic sleeve. "I took the liberty of printing one off before I left home. I thought it unlikely that a small town lawyer would have encountered a client in need of my services before."

"Small town—" He sat back and folded his arms. "That's— thoughtful of you. Thanks."

She'd swear his mouth tipped up in the beginnings of a grin. Was he laughing at her? A flicker of anger ignited within her. Anna had experience of lawyers with no sense of humour— patronising men who'd treated her like a performing child when she interpreted for her parents in the court case after their break in.

When they turned a vicious assault on her family into little more than a misdemeanour.

Eyeing Jack Donaldson as she slid the form across the table, she wondered, *was he like those other lawyers*? Would it make the coming interview more difficult if she demanded to know what he thought was so funny?

He put his glasses on and filled in his details in blue ink. Her section was already complete in regulation black ink. She watched him sign the form, usually her first clue to the personality and attitude of those she worked with. His signature was legible with no oversized capital letters that experience had taught her went with an overbearing ego. Giving him points for that, she waited as he checked the form, signed the page she would keep for her records, clicked his pen shut and pushed his glasses up onto his head.

"So, any tips to make it easier for me to give my client what he needs?"

"You're asking me for tips?" Aware that her jaw had dropped, she closed her mouth and sat.

"You're the expert here so—anything I should be aware of?"

The lawyer's request had thrown her off balance. Had she been so antsy about his profession before her parents' case? Maybe he was a decent man. Reserving judgement for the time being, she set her hands palm down on the table top. "Speak to Kaden, not me. He'll probably be proficient at lip-reading. You don't need to speak extra slowly or loudly, but it will help if you enunciate clearly. That will help him to work out what you're saying by the shapes your mouth makes. Treat him as you would any other client. I'm here only to facilitate communication between you."

"Thanks."

A knock on the door heralded the constable carrying a takeaway cup Anna recognised as coming from Darcy's bakery café. The constable handed the cup to Jack with a "Great idea", before Kaden appeared in the doorway escorted by Sergeant Edwards. The senior officer pushed Kaden into the chair beside Anna with a heavy hand on his shoulder. The boy stumbled and fell against Anna's shoulder.

Edwards unlocked one hand from the handcuffs and locked the other cuff to a sturdy anchor point in the middle of the table. As he stepped back, he spoke to Jack and ignored Anna. "We'll be right outside if he causes any trouble."

Anger vibrated through Anna's body, but she forced her voice to remain level. "Sergeant, please remove the handcuffs completely."

Dull red filled Edwards' face, a close match for the red trails in his eyes. "Not after the way he behaved this morning. He isn't safe out of cuffs."

"He can't sign if he can't use both hands."

Jack pushed his chair back and stood. "Sergeant, please release my client. Locking the door will secure your prisoner, but I can't agree to anything that will prejudice his ability to fully communicate with us."

Surprised by his unequivocal support, Anna had an inappropriate urge to cheer. Instead, she met his eyes and nodded. "I'm agreeable to working under those conditions."

Outnumbered, the sergeant huffed, put his hands on his hips, and then shook his head. "It's on your heads if he goes wild again." He unlocked the handcuffs and then left without another word. The sound of a key turning was loud in the silence of the room.

Jack rubbed his hands together and their gazes met again. "Right, let's get on with the interview. I need to see both of you and you need to see Kaden. Where should we all sit to make this easy?"

"Stay where you are. I'll establish his name and tell him how this will operate. I'll speak aloud so you know what I'm signing and then translate his answers." Anna turned her chair to face the teenager and signed, *What's your name?*

Kaden.

Kaden who?

The boy shook his head.

Okay, we'll come back to that later. This man is Jack Donaldson and he has offered to be your lawyer. He's going to make sure you get proper legal representation. Do you agree to him acting for you?

Do you trust him?

How should she answer that when she'd only just met Jack? All she had to go on was his action in support of her. Was that enough by itself to indicate trustworthiness? As her hands lay still in her lap, Kaden shifted in his seat and cast an anxious look her way.

"Anna, what did he say?" Jack's question reminded her she hadn't passed on the boy's last question.

"He asked if I trust you."

"Are you hesitating because you don't know me, or is there something you haven't told me? If it's any help, I believe I have a pretty good reputation for honesty and fairness."

She nodded at Jack and signed, *I think so.*

Kaden stared at Jack, who met his eyes with a steady gaze that inspired Anna to believe him. *For the time being at least.*

She touched Kaden's hand. *Yes, I trust him.*

Okay. What does he want to know?

She turned to Jack. "Your turn. What do you want to ask?"

Jack spoke to the teenager. "Tell me what happened this morning, and why it happened."

Anna translated, but Kaden's hands flew as he told his story, simply and factually. *I was hungry, hadn't eaten for two days. Open door, nice smell in kitchen. Took muffins.* He gave her an impish grin. *Really good muffins.*

Jack was typing notes—touch typing, she noted—but at that he stopped. "He's talking about your cooking I take it? What sort of muffins?"

"Banana and blueberry."

"My favourite. Go on."

Nobody around on farm. Wanted an egg. Farmer came and locked me in with chooks. Police came, and you.

Jack typed on his tablet, hit the return key, and looked at Kaden. "Okay, so you were hungry and took food. Did you take anything else?"

Angry slashing gestures reinforced his reply. *Not a thief. Hungry.*

"But you went into a house, and onto property that wasn't yours, and took food that wasn't yours to eat. Under the law, that's theft, following breaking and entering, regardless of how hungry you were. Of course, a magistrate might treat you with leniency if food was all you took."

Not a thief.

Anna signed as she told Jack, "He didn't take anything else, not from my cottage."

Jack covered his mouth, hiding his words from the boy. "It would probably make a difference if you chose not to press charges. Is that something you might consider?"

Anna's gaze flicked between Kaden and Jack, and back to the boy. He seemed so young, so skinny. *Why did you come to Lark Creek? Where do you live? How old are you?*

Not wanted at home.

Her sympathy for the boy stalled. Was he simply a rebellious teen or was there abuse of some kind? *Tell me more.*

Kicked out.

Where do you live?

Kaden's head drooped and he rested his elbows on his knees. His fingers, so active moments earlier, hung like dead twigs between his legs.

She touched one knee lightly. *How old are you?*

Seventeen.

Older than Anna had thought. With a sigh, she turned to Jack. "I'll think about your suggestion, but we need to find where his parents are. He seems reluctant to tell us where they live, or his surname."

"Somewhere, someone will be missing him. I'll ask Constable Brooks to check the police database for a missing person's report."

Kaden jumped to his feet, sounds of distress falling from his mouth. Frantically he pleaded with emphatic gestures, *Don't ask. Dangerous. He'll kill me.*

Anna set both hands on the boy's thin shoulders and spoke carefully. "It's okay, stop, no one will hurt you here."

"What's he saying?" Jack was on his feet and moved quickly to her side. His arm came up in front of her and he took hold of the boy's shoulder. "What's wrong?"

She stepped back and signed, *Stay calm. No one will hurt you here.*

.Wide eyes, full of fear and mistrust, flicked between her and Jack. When Jack had eased him back into his chair and Kaden's full attention was on her, she spoke and signed, *Who will kill you?*

Jack's startled gaze changed quickly into understanding. "It's okay, mate. We won't do anything to put you in danger."

Kaden signed, *My uncle. I saw . . . something. Don't tell him I'm here.*

She stared into Jack's concerned eyes. "He says he saw something and now his uncle will kill him."

Chapter 4

Jack chugged the last of his coffee and set the takeaway cup beside his tablet. Late afternoon sun slanted through the high windows in a splash of autumn warmth as he checked the document one final time and then hit the send button. He removed his glasses and rubbed his eyes. "It's done."

Anna's hands stilled as though in white-knuckled prayer. "And your friend in Brisbane—you trust him to be completely discreet in his enquiries?"

"Yes. In the meantime, Kaden is safe in Lark Creek."

"Will the police keep him in a cell? He's only seventeen and—" She was working hard to keep her anxiety under wraps, but the frazzled edges were wearing thin. As the hours had dragged past and she refused to leave in case he needed her to translate for Kaden, she'd wilted over the table. Three tiny freckles on her nose that he hadn't noticed this morning stood out against her pale skin, but it was the shadows beneath her eyes, and the strained anxiety in their depths that puzzled him.

"I've sent an urgent request for a case manager to look after him, but budget cuts have cut out a lot of funding."

"He can't stay in jail!" Tired as she was, she came out fighting on the boy's behalf. He admired that about her, the desire to seek justice for the youth who had broken into her home only hours before. "We've got to do something."

"I've arranged to appear before the circuit magistrate this evening. It's unusual, but she agreed because of the nature of the case and Kaden's particular situation." Grateful he'd made a connection with Judy Overhill before she joined the court as a circuit judge, he decided not to share that detail.

"Will the magistrate release him?"

"Maybe, but without a case manager, Kaden's got nowhere to go."

Even as the words left his mouth, Anna's eyes lost their focus. Where did she go when she zoned out like that? Her lips parted and her tongue touched the corner of her mouth, just as it had when she entered the police station this morning. When he'd sensed her unease and she'd frozen him out—was that her nervous 'tell'?

"If it's only a case of finding him a temporary home . . ." Both hands spread flat on the table. "Maybe he could stay in my spare bedroom."

"The court probably wouldn't agree to that."

"Why not? I've made the offer."

And what an offer it was. Priding himself on his sense of justice, still Jack was certain he wouldn't have made the same offer to anyone who'd just broken into his home—youth or adult. He shook his head.

"First of all, you haven't been vetted for such care situations; second, Kaden broke into your home and stole from you. The magistrate is likely to deem that a conflict of interest."

Anna opened her mouth to object and he held up one hand.

"These are facts, Anna. There is also a query I would pose regarding your emotional state in the wake of the break-in." He'd stake his pending partnership on there being more to Anna's seesawing emotions throughout the day than Kaden's intrusion in her home.

"What do you mean? I'm fine."

"You were as tense as a piano wire when you walked in here this morning, and carrying a chip on your shoulder when you met me. I don't need to know your personal business, but I'd ask you to think carefully about what you'd be taking on, even temporarily."

As she glared at him, her body sat up straight and a fire

appeared in her eyes. "Okay. I'll grant I don't like lawyers much, not since—" Her next breath was audible, agitated and swift on the way in, slow and deliberately controlled on the way out. "But let me ask you this. Who in this town can communicate with Kaden the way I can? I don't know of another person who signs. Maybe you should tell your magistrate that."

Brushing a thumb over his lower lip, Jack thought about her comment. While he was pretty sure Kaden could lip-read well, he hadn't spoken at all, which would make things difficult for any non-signing carer. "You make an important point. I'm not convinced though. If I were to suggest your solution to the magistrate, do you have any idea of what you would be taking on?"

A sharp nod, lips pressed together . . . Her gaze met and held his. "I understand, more than you know."

One day, Jack wanted to find out what had shaped Anna Wilkins. That she might be as vulnerable as his young client was clear, but beneath her freckles and soft brown eyes, he'd seen glimpses of a keen intelligence and a fighting spirit prepared to take on the court and all its judicial power in defence of the boy.

"In that case, will you tell that to the judge in court? I think hearing it from you might reassure the magistrate about your suitability, if she grants bail."

***

Court, speaking on behalf of Kaden . . .

Memories rose like a king tide, crashed over her and stole her voice as she processed Jack's request. Her mother's incoherent cries as the home invasion shattered her world; her unintelligible attempts to speak when the horrible defence lawyer pushed her into a quivering mess of humiliation. Not even Anna's presence beside her mother on the witness stand had been enough to calm her. The fact the lawyer had been reprimanded after she'd complained about his bullying behaviour to the State Law Society hadn't helped her mother.

But if Anna didn't attend now, didn't speak for Kaden, who would? If a case manager couldn't be found at short notice—and Jack didn't seem to hold much hope on that score—would the frightened teenager be kept in the cells?

"I'll present my case."

"Thank you." He sounded sincere, and something in his voice, some thread that sounded like compassion held her attention until his hand lightly settled over hers. Her death-grip on the strap of her satchel loosened as she recognised how cold her hands were beneath his.

"It's little enough to do for him."

"It's everything to him right now. I can't begin to imagine how scared he's been since he ran away. Fearing someone in your own family wants to kill you would be terrible for anyone, but the fact he can't hear, can't speak to most people—" He shook his head and looked her in the eyes. "Anna, I promise you I'll do everything in my power to help him."

Tipping her head, her gaze sought the truth on his face. Reading people's subconscious reactions was second nature in her work. Words had power, but words could deceive. One's body wasn't as easily controlled. Seeing only sincerity in his eyes, she nodded. "You really mean that, don't you?" Was it possible Jack was one of the decent ones, a man who did what he said he would? Hope flickered like a candle in the darkness she'd hidden in for a year.

"Yes." He gently squeezed her hands before pushing his chair back. "I'll let the officers know what's happening. Maybe Constable Brooks will drive us to court. She might be happy to get in a bit of overtime."

Once the subdued tones of two voices filtered through the door, Anna put her head down on her hands, giving her body a few moments to react in private, unhindered by her need to appear strong in front of everyone, even Jack who had been kinder than she had expected. *He's a lawyer*, she reminded herself.

I couldn't help you, Mum, but I'll help Kaden, no matter what.

Chapter 5

". . . and so, Your Honour, given the nature of the threats Kaden claims have been made against him, and in consideration of both his youth and his hearing impairment, we submit that Ms Wilkins is the only real option for short term, temporary care of Kaden."

Judge Overhill peered over her glasses at Anna and Jack held his breath. It was up to Anna now to convince the magistrate she was the best person to take responsibility for the boy.

"Ms Wilkins, your credentials are excellent and I accept that your blue card is, in this case, sufficient for a temporary position to be considered. Kaden's needs must be addressed in the best possible care situation. However, I note you were personally affected by a violent home invasion a year ago."

Jack sucked back a gasp and gritted his teeth.

Why hadn't Anna told him? Damn it, how could he do his best for his client when key information was withheld?

He sat back and folded his arms. It wouldn't help if Judy Overhill realised he hadn't known about Anna's past, but he'd have a few choice words to say to Anna when they got out of here.

Full and open communication for a start!

As he watched, Anna's throat rippled. Beneath the stark lighting of the courtroom, her face was pale, but she stood straight and met the judge with a direct gaze. "Your Honour, the two instances are completely different. I wasn't present when Kaden entered my home, and all he took was food. If your concern is that I might be suffering from shock after this morning's incident, let me assure you that's not the case."

She turned slightly towards the boy and began signing as she spoke to the magistrate. "I believe I'm the most suitable choice to care for Kaden's special needs while investigations are carried out into his claims about his uncle. He signs, but doesn't vocalise, he lip-reads, although to what extent I haven't been able to ascertain, except that he seems to require signing to clarify things sometimes. His first interaction with the police was alarming, to say the least, and both his physical and emotional well-being would be better served if he were to stay with someone—me—who can communicate with him, and who cares."

The magistrate made a note on her file and looked up. "Ask Kaden now if he's prepared to accept you as his carer for the next two weeks."

As often as Jack had watched Anna in action today, the speed and grace of her signing still surprised him. Her face came alive as she communicated in a language he'd never thought about, one which calmed and connected a deaf teenager with the world of sound.

Kaden tapped the index finger of his right hand between his left thumb and first finger three times in the signed 'Yes' that had become familiar to Jack as the day wore on. The teenager looked at the judge, nodded and repeated the word with three taps that Jack heard.

The magistrate smiled. "Yes, young man. You don't need to shout. I understand you're willing to accept Ms Wilkins' supervision. Let it be so ordered."

For the first time since Jack had met Anna, her face relaxed into a small smile. For the magistrate and for the boy. She didn't meet Jack's eyes, but that didn't matter. They'd achieved what they'd set out to get. Relief and a sense of accomplishment raced through Jack's mind. He bowed his head to the magistrate. "Thank you, Your Honour. We appreciate you seeing us so late."

"When it's important, we all go the extra mile, Mr Donaldson. Good evening." She rose from behind the bench and exited through a door in the panelled wood wall, unnoticeable if you weren't looking for it.

Constable Brooks rose from the front row of public seats. "Great. On the way back to Lark Creek, do you want to stop and grab a burger?"

***

Anna sat beside Kaden in the back of the police car, glad of the inky darkness of a moonless night. Twin beams of light illuminated the road, but in the back of the car, night draped her like a blanket. Kaden sat still, his presence, a slight rustle of clothing when he moved. She was grateful he couldn't sign in the dark; she needed time to mentally prepare for his presence in her home—*did I really offer to take him in?*

In the front seats, Jack chatted with Marion Brooks, but Anna tried to block out their conversation. Her thoughts circled, chased one another like a fox after a hare.

Taking in the thief who had broken into her home was inviting danger . . .

Leaving a vulnerable deaf boy in the cells was wrong . . .

No, it was the right thing to do. Her mother would approve of her decision, but still Anna's heartbeat galloped at the idea of inviting Kaden into her home.

PTSD, the psychiatrist had told her, *a natural result of the trauma of the violence she had been subjected to.*

The assault had scarred all of them, whether the scars showed or not. She'd thought time away from the family home—time and moving to a tiny country town—would have helped her achieve calm. But unquiet thoughts buzzed through her brain like a swarm of bees until she wanted to jump out of the moving vehicle and run screaming down the road.

At last, the constable turned into the driveway along the western side of Lark Creek police station and parked beneath the single security light.

Anna reached for the door handle and jerked it. Nothing.

She pulled again, her other hand feeling for a release lock. Her lungs constricted as she tugged, to no avail. "I can't get out."

Perhaps Jack heard the note of panic in her voice. "I'll open it for you, hang on." He jumped out of his seat and pulled her door open.

She stepped out quickly, stumbling in her haste to escape the confines of the car. Another leftover from the home invasion, her claustrophobia hadn't been a problem since she'd moved into the cottage, but the metallic smell of the cage, and other non-specific odours beneath the smell of air freshener had triggered the primal need to escape. Her legs wobbled like jelly and she tipped her head, breathing deeply of the scent of a flowering gum hanging over the side fence. "Thanks." Travelling to court in the front seat, she hadn't noticed that feature first time around.

Marion Brooks' voice came from the other side of the vehicle where she opened Kaden's door. "Sorry, Anna. The rear doors can't be opened from the inside. It's a safety feature, like kid-safe locks on family cars."

"I'm fine. So, what's next? Do I have to sign more forms or can I just head home with Kaden?"

Marion appeared at her side, one hand beneath Kaden's elbow. "One signature and you can go home. It's been a long day for everyone."

"Stopping for a burger was a good idea, Marion. Thanks." Jack closed both doors on the passenger side of the car and waited for the officer to click the remote lock. Yellow indicator lights flashed and the distinctive click confirmed the vehicle was locked.

Marion led the way up the back steps and through the kitchen, past the cells and back to the interview room. "Take a seat. I'll only be a minute."

Anna explained brief details to Kaden who slumped into a chair. Was it too much to hope that Jack Donaldson would leave his questions about her previous encounter with a home invader alone?

She risked a quick glance his way. Back in the courtroom, his frown had made his displeasure with her clear. Up until the magistrate's question, Anna had hoped to keep her past as her secret, to not allow it to define her. Clearly the magistrate had researched her credentials thoroughly before they appeared before her.

As she had to.

But not mentioning it to Jack before he heard it from the magistrate seemed to have affected the tentative trust they'd established over the course of the day.

He watched her from beneath straight eyebrows that underlined his frown.

She waited. It was strange how their roles had reversed since this morning. Then it had been her who had distrusted him. Now . . .

"Are you still okay with the plan now the magistrate has agreed, or are you having second thoughts? Because I was thinking, if you have any concerns about being in your home alone with Kaden, you could both move into my place."

The offer came out of left field, so far off what she'd expected him to say it didn't immediately register in her frazzled brain. "Your place?"

"I'm renting a three-bedroom house on Leonard Drive, not far from Rose Cottage. If you're worried about being alone and living out of town, that is."

She looked at Kaden. He was watching Jack's mouth as he made the offer. When Jack finished speaking, Kaden hunched his shoulders and turned away.

Jack's gaze darted to the teenager. "What's wrong?"

She touched Kaden's shoulder. He jerked away from her touch. With a shake of her head towards Jack, Anna moved until she was kneeling in front of Kaden. *What's wrong?*

I frightened you. Sorry. Feel bad. Please let me stay with you. I want to stay with you.

Just with me? Jack offered his home.

Not with him. Just you.

Her gaze connected with Jack's. "Kaden wants to stay with me at the cottage. We'll be fine there, but thanks for your kind offer."

Marion entered and set a duplicate form on the table. She pointed to a box near the bottom of the page. "Sign here and here please, Anna, and then you can go. It's late, and we can sort out everything else in the morning."

Anna scribbled her signature, picked up her satchel and stood. "We'll be on our way then. Good night." She beckoned Kaden. He came to her side, tucking in behind her shoulder as though, even now, the long arm of the law might return him to the cells.

Jack took a copy of the form and tucked it inside a file. "I'll be in touch in the morning, Anna. Thanks for what you're doing for Kaden. And will you tell him please—" He extended a hand across the table. "Kaden, Anna has gone out of her way to help you. It's up to you to show her she was right about you."

The teenager flicked a glance at Anna's hands confirming the message before he nodded and shook Jack's hand. He followed her through the doorway and out to her car.

Chapter 6

Night pressed close as Jack sat on his front steps and took the top off a beer. He drank slowly, savouring the slide of cold liquid down his throat while his eyes adjusted to the darkness.

Today had been—unexpected, interesting, challenging in ways he'd never have encountered in the Brisbane law office. Working in the business law section of the national firm, he wouldn't have touched criminal work, or become the default representative of a juvenile thief. Nor would he have made the acquaintance of a woman like Anna Wilkins.

The women he worked with wore tailored suits and stilettoes and, like everyone else in the firm, they were intent on climbing the corporate ladder. The prize of a partnership after long years of fifteen-hour working days kept them all on the treadmill—himself included.

The position in Lark Creek was a favour—taking over the declining practice of the retiring uncle of one of the partners and giving the firm a foothold in this region. The work here was both simpler and more varied than what he'd been doing, but Jack had seen it as a tacit nod; he was the frontrunner for the next partnership in the firm. All he had to do was build up the rural practice, incorporate it into the parent company, and return to one of the second top floor offices.

He leaned against the upright post and tipped the bottle to his mouth. The dark outline of O'Reilly's Ridge was just visible against a midnight-blue sky, and a scattering of stars patterned the dark canvas. A pinpoint of light flashed from the ridge and then vanished. Rick Peyton had mentioned his father still lived up on the ridge, even after discovering the son he'd never known was living at the foot of his mountain. *Graham must be out checking his traps.*

Jack liked the outdoors, not to the extent that he'd enjoy living under canvas permanently, but enough to appreciate the ex-army veteran's choice suited him.

Bet he sees everything that goes on in town from up there.

Beside Jack on the step, his phone pinged with an incoming message. The sound and the knowledge it would be about work shattered his goal of relaxing for what was left of the evening. Maybe he should turn it off and ignore it until morning?

His inclination was to shut the world out for a few hours. His thumb hovered over the button, drawn to switch the device into sleep mode despite the message sitting on the screen, black on white, and he couldn't deny the siren call to know what it said. Reading between its lines spelled the end of any hope of switching off.

You won't believe what I've found on preliminary search for Kaden Roscoe's family. Call me ASAP. Smithy.

"Shit." The word erupted out of him, disturbing unseen birds in the tree at the corner of the yard. They squawked in displeasure as he pushed to his feet and strode inside, already scrolling through his contacts.

Smithy picked up after a single ring. "Your client, the Roscoe kid? If he's seen anything and is on the run because of it, it's big."

Jack flicked the switch on his desk lamp and pulled a note pad and pen towards him. "Tell me what you know."

"This uncle you mentioned the kid is afraid of . . . It's Ferdy Hickman."

"Hickman? The crime boss on the police's top ten most wanted list?" Jack's gut clenched as the implications crashed around him.

"Yep, one and the same. If your kid comes forward and tells us what he knows, we have a real chance to put Hickman away this time."

"Kaden's scared. And if he's been caught up in Hickman's activities—if he actually meant it when he said his uncle would kill him . . ." Jack's mind raced, and he began scribbling a list of urgent actions.

"I'll need to come out and interview him, find out what he claims to know and see if it tallies with Hickman's recent activity."

"Maybe start your investigation in Brisbane. We think Kaden ran away from his uncle's house, but he's reluctant to say more than what I sent you."

"We? You working with someone else out there? And I thought I was your one and only contact."

"Kaden is hearing-impaired. He doesn't speak, just signs. When the police picked him up this morning for B and E, the neighbour helped. She's an Auslan interpreter. You'll need her assistance. The boy is staying with her."

"Motherly type? I'll charm her into helping, don't worry."

Motherly was the last word that came to Jack's mind as he thought of Anna and the slim body that had emerged from her loose cardigan when Marion had turned the heater on. She was an attractive woman, not his type, but definitely not motherly, despite her protective instincts flaring when it looked like Kaden might be spending a night in the cells. "Good luck with that."

"What. Dragon, is she?"

"You'll see when you get here, but Smithy, if Hickman is the boy's uncle and Kaden knows something big, they'll both be in danger."

"I'll organise witness protection immediately. Sit tight, mate."

The screen went dark and Jack sat back in his chair. Allowing Anna to take responsibility for Kaden had put her in a dangerous position, one that he wasn't sure she was equipped to deal with. It was one thing to offer to care for the deaf teenager. Facing up to his gangster uncle wasn't part of the deal, especially when he suspected she was still suffering emotional distress after the first home invasion Judy Overhill had mentioned.

He picked up the phone to call her, warn her . . . eleven p.m. flashed up on the screen. With a huff of disgust, he tossed the phone down. Let her have a good night's sleep first. Then early tomorrow morning, he'd visit her cottage and lay out a plan.

All he had to do was come up with a good one to keep her and the boy under the radar until Smithy arranged a better alternative. *That was some tall order.*

He snorted and began mind-mapping possibilities on the note pad.

***

Anna woke to sounds of heavy knocking on her back door. Gritty-eyed and groggy from too little sleep, she stumbled into the kitchen, still tying the sash of her robe as she peered through the glass panel and screen door beyond at Jack's face. She unlocked the back door and stepped onto the small, screened back veranda.

"Good morning. Do you always make social calls at sparrow-fart times, or am I getting special treatment, because if that's the case—"

"We need to talk, Anna."

Like a cold shower his words and that serious tone in his voice chilled her. She turned the lock, little more than a token at best, and stepped to one side. "You'd better come inside then. I'll put the kettle on for coffee."

"Thanks." He set an orange manila folder on the white-painted table and pulled out a chair. The legs scraped on the wooden floor, and the sound sent goose bumps marching down her spine as she filled the kettle and set it to boil.

"Should I wake Kaden?"

"Later. I need to talk to you first."

"Fire away." She spooned coffee into two mugs, spilling a few grains on the bench top.

"I contacted a friend of mine who's moving up the ranks in

the Federal Police yesterday. He was able to do a preliminary check on Kaden's story for me. It's not good."

Anna perched on the edge of the chair and faced Jack. "Do you mean Kaden lied to us to get out of trouble?"

"Worse than that, Anna. Kaden told us the truth."

"I'm confused. How can telling the truth be worse than him lying to us?"

"The uncle he said would kill him if he found him? He's on the police top ten most wanted list."

The chill of the tiles on her bare feet was nothing compared to the ice that filled her veins. "A criminal?"

"The leader of a notorious gang wanted for questioning in several murders, extortion and more. My friend Smithy wants to question Kaden this afternoon."

"Murder . . . what has that poor boy seen?" She looked into Jack's eyes, surprised to find him watching her intently. "Do you think Kaden is in danger?"

"Smithy is organising for Kaden to go into a witness protection programme."

"I see. So all our efforts last night only bought him one night out of the cells."

"That's one way of looking at it. I'm guessing he hasn't woken yet?"

She shook her head. "Will your friend take him back to jail until they find a place for him?"

Jack shrugged. "I've no idea where they'll place him, although I doubt he'll be going into a jail cell. The protection programme has never featured in any of my cases. Small town lawyer, remember." The ghost of a grin flickered across his mouth before he opened the folder and drew out the top sheet. "I suspect today's news will nullify the agreement you signed last night, but I wanted to prepare you in case Smithy decides to push it."

"What part of the agreement do you see as a problem?"

"Well, you agreed to be Kaden's carer for a period of two

weeks beginning yesterday. It's possible Smithy might ask you to accompany Kaden into hiding while they work out another alternative."

She slapped her hands on the table and pushed to her feet. Her empty stomach clenched. "They want me to go into hiding with him?"

He held up both hands. "I'm not saying it will happen, but I wanted to forewarn you about the possibility Smithy could ask for that."

The kettle began whistling. Working on autopilot, Anna switched it off and poured water onto coffee in two mugs. She set both on the table, sat, and sipped hers, black and bitter and oh-so-necessary to break through the weird trance she'd slipped into.

Putting the mug down, she kept both hands wrapped around it. "Okay, so your friend might ask me to go into witness protection to communicate with Kaden. Or he might not."

"On balance, I don't think it will be likely. Look, I raised it because I didn't want you to get a huge shock if it came up later. I figured it's better to have time to think calmly and rationally, which is tough when you're under pressure to answer straightaway."

She looked around her rustic kitchen—the railway clock, mantelpiece, black slow combustion stove . . . the photo of her with her parents on a holiday at the coast when she'd been younger than Kaden. If Jack's friend asked it of her, what would she be leaving? Nice as the cottage was, it wasn't home.

It was a bolthole for a rabbit afraid to face the world. Afraid to live.

"I'm sorry, Anna. I didn't mean to alarm you."

"You didn't, or maybe only a little. Maybe this is the wake up call I needed. Look, if it comes to the push, I'd prefer to go with Kaden. He needs me."

***

Jack paced the length of the back veranda, waiting for

Smithy to pick up his call. Anna was unexpected and unusual. *Admirable Anna.* The name popped into his head as Smithy answered.

"Well, what did Dragon Lady say?"

"She's made of stern stuff. If I were you, I'd be on my best behaviour, mate."

"She's agreed to help with Kaden's interview? Excellent. Never doubted your ability to get her to agree. Next step will be to convince her to—"

"Already done."

"What?"

"Anna agreed to accompany Kaden into a witness protection location if needed. She's connected with him and, given what you'll be asking him about his uncle, I think a friendly face will be helpful. She agrees."

"Does she understand that she'll have to leave her home and family, friends—without telling a soul?"

"She's only been in Lark Creek for a few months. Less than a year I think. Tends to keep to herself, although a few locals know she paints. I gather she's done a few commissions here and there."

"Hmm, might open up a few more options for us. I'll get a flight to the closest airport and then hire a car. Text me the address, will you?"

Jack sent Anna's address as he continued talking. "I feel responsible for them both. Maybe I'll hang around here until you arrive, just to be on the safe side."

"See yourself as a dragon slayer, do you? Thanks for that. Oh, and tell your lady to pack a bag for herself so we can move her and the boy at short notice." Smithy rang off without saying a goodbye. But then their next conversation he'd continue as though there hadn't been a break. That was Smithy—no BS, just action.

Jack tapped the phone against his palm before sliding it into his pocket and joining Anna in the kitchen. Kaden was sitting in the chair where Jack had been. The teenager was bare-chested and wearing cartoon sheep-patterned sleep trousers Jack suspected belonged to Anna. He'd also showered and washed his hair, and looked less like a frightened child than he had yesterday.

Kaden looked up. His hands moved in a quick gesture, touching first his stomach and then his chest.

Jack shook his head. "I don't know what that means, mate. You're hungry?"

"Kaden said good morning to you." Anna made the same sign, but slowly. "This is how you return his greeting."

Jack's attempt at copying her drew a grin from Kaden. He signed something more complex and Anna laughed.

"He said he's the expert in silent communication, but to watch him and learn."

"Good idea." Jack smiled and gave a thumbs up gesture, hoping it didn't translate as something rude in Kaden's world. "But before we continue my education in signing, I should share the plan for today."

Jack explained about Smithy and the interview, taking care to speak to Kaden. The boy's gaze flicked across to Anna each time Jack paused between sentences, nodding as the importance of revealing what he knew was made clear.

Mention of the witness programme drew a frown and a flare of his nostrils, and a flurry of gestures back and forth gave Jack no real clue, other than that Kaden appeared reluctant about the idea. His agreement was slow in coming, confined to a single, sharp nod. Mutiny lurked—in the muscle jumping in his tight jaw and the steely look in his eyes.

"He'll think about it if he has to, but he isn't keen on the idea." Anna's gaze clung to Kaden's face for several heartbeats.

One day of watching the pair of them converse had given Jack a sense of the spoken length of signed question and answer. Anna and the boy's exchange had said far more than Anna translated. Was it worth pushing, or better to leave it to Anna's discretion?

"Understood. Let's leave that aspect aside for now. Is there anything else either of you want to know?" Anna might fill him in later. At least, he could ask. He'd just have to accept her answer.

Kaden shook his head and hoed into the pile of toast cooling on his plate.

Anna set her elbow on the table and leaned her cheek on her hand, turning slightly away. Jack figured it was so Kaden couldn't lip-read their exchange. "Did you tell your friend I'm willing to stay with Kaden for the time being?"

"Yes. He's pleased by your offer. Grateful too, I imagine, if he's capable of thinking of people as humans rather than chess pieces."

"That doesn't sound as though you like him very much. I thought he was your friend?"

"Don't get me wrong, we've been friends since uni days, but Smithy can be blunt and so focused on his goal he doesn't worry about other people's sensibilities. I'm used to him."

Anna frowned and interlaced her fingers. "Jack, I know you think I'm—weak for running away to the country after what happened to me, to my family."

"I never said that. In fact—"

She held up a hand and he shut up. "Not in so many words. I saw it in your eyes when the magistrate asked about the other break in. Maybe it *was* weakness of a sort, but I'm not some hothouse flower you have to coddle. Agreeing to take responsibility for Kaden was like waking from a long sleep filled with nightmarish creatures and discovering the world wasn't as big and bad as I'd let myself believe. There are things I can do, ways I can fight back. Helping Kaden isn't just about him. It's a way of empowering myself again. Can you understand what I'm saying?"

A shaft of embarrassed guilt shot through him. Even his offer to stay—which he hadn't shared with her yet—might appear to be coddling in her view. But the memory of a prickly, feisty woman desperately trying not to reveal how anxious she was had touched him. "Anna, let me put it on record here and now—I know you're a strong-minded woman and I'm sorry I doubted you for one second. I won't underestimate you again."

"Thanks. I just wanted to be clear." She pushed her chair back and went to the toaster. "Do you have time for breakfast before you go in to work?"

He rubbed the back of his neck. Crunch time. "If it's okay with you, I thought I'd stick around until Smithy gets here."

Her hands hit her hips and her gaze pinned him. "Did you not hear a word I said?"

"It's not about you."

"Don't give me that BS it's-not-about-you-it's-me line."

"Honestly. I've got work with me and I'd rather be here when Smithy arrives. He has a habit of appearing when you least expect him. It'll be easier if I'm not in the middle of a client conference at the office when he gets here."

She sucked in an audible breath and her tongue touched the corner of her mouth as it had yesterday. In that time before he'd discovered they were caught up with a criminal who wanted to kill his client . . .

Us too, if he ever finds Kaden.

"Is there something you're not telling me? Some other reason why you want to stay?" Fierce intelligence burned in her narrowed eyes, a look that put him on notice. Anna Wilkins would not accept help readily, and if that help came from misguided chivalry . . .

Was that what he was doing—trying to make like a white knight?

"Are we already in danger and you're not telling us?"

"No." The word burst from him with the weight of unexpressed fears propelling it louder than he intended. Kaden stopped chewing and looked first at him and then at Anna. She shook her head.

Take it down a notch.

"No," he repeated more conversationally. "Call me a worrier, but I got you into this and I'll feel better—" He stabbed his thumb towards his chest. "*Me*, Anna. I'll feel better if I'm here with you, okay?"

Chapter 7

Anna tossed her paintbrush into the jar of water and reached for the clips holding the watercolour in place. Usually the act of creating calmed her, but Jack's evasive response had set her nerves jumping and the view from her front veranda had transformed into a dark and dangerous landscape, one in which she could imagine men with guns, with intent to kill, lurking behind bushes.

"That's really good, Anna."

Jack's voice so close behind startled her. "Damn it, why are you creeping up on me?"

"Hey, don't blame me if you were miles away in your art." He shoved both hands in his pockets and stepped back, his gaze falling on her painting. He tipped his head to the side and frowned. "You've transformed the view into something else, like out of a dream, maybe."

Wrapping her arms around her waist, Anna tried to see it through Jack's eyes. "More of a nightmare I'd say. I was going to scrap it, but maybe you're right about the transformative nature of art—"

"As opposed to it being representative?"

"It's more to do with ways of seeing the world than capturing a photographic likeness. For instance, the way the lowest branch on that tree is bowed towards the ground could be transformed into a crouching monster—" Her words dried up, lodged in her throat; her finger frozen in the act of pointing.

A nondescript mid-sized car turned into her driveway and headed up the slope past the dam towards the cottage. A plume of dirt hung in the still air, like the tail of an exotic bird.

"Is that your friend?" Sharp tones and choppy breaths—she had to disguise her nerves better than that if Smithy was to believe she'd be a fit guardian for the boy.

Jack peered through a narrow gap in the sheer curtains. "It's Smithy, and it looks like he's come alone."

The driver parked the car in a clear area behind the olive and wattle trees where it would be unseen from the road. A tall man unwound himself from the driver's seat, stood and stretched before opening the passenger door and taking out a briefcase.

Anna leaned around Jack's arm, trying to see without being seen. A faint scent of olives rose from his skin. *Soap? Or had he had a close encounter with her olive grove?* "Now what?"

"We could start by letting him in. How about that?" One side of Jack's mouth tipped up and he stepped around her and went to the back door.

Anna followed him as far as the kitchen, but some instinct made her hang back. What kind of man was Jack's friend? Tentative trust in Jack wasn't sufficient basis for accepting his friend on a say-so. Not when their lives could depend on the decisions he was about to make on their behalf.

Anna avoided lip-reading as far as possible, unless she was working as an interpreter. Did what she was doing for Kaden count as work, or self-preservation? Before she could talk herself out of it, she stepped to one side of the window and watched as *Smithy* shook Jack's hand.

All quiet on the western front then? Smithy looked around, the slow turn of his head belying the sharpness of his gaze.

Nothing out of the ordinary.

And Dragon Lady's still agreeable to the protection idea?

Anna blinked, unsure whether to be affronted or to laugh. When had she become *Dragon Lady*, for there was nobody else Jack's friend could mean? And what had she done to deserve that label?

Jack's answer was lost as he turned and looked up at the

slopes of O'Reilly's Ridge.

Let's meet her and the boy then. Smithy followed Jack onto the veranda and into the kitchen.

As they came through the open doorway, Anna was busying herself at the sink, filling the kettle. She set it down and ran her hands down her jeans.

"Anna Wilkins, meet Agent Charles Smith."

Anna held out her hand. "Charles? I'd like to say it's a pleasure to meet you, but under the circumstances—"

"True. Not pleasant knowing you might have a crime boss on your tail. Thanks for offering to translate, but are you sure you're qualified? Old son here misled me about your age."

Anna folded her arms and looked at him with the Lauren Bacall look she'd worked on for a high school play, chin down and peering up sideways. It gave her the confidence to call him out. "As in—you expected Dragon Lady to be ancient and decrepit and have long red nails?"

Smithy guffawed and Jack jumped in, a dull red flush staining his cheeks. "I didn't say anything about a dragon, or your age. That was all Smithy's creation."

"I like her, mate. Okay, you'll do, Anna, but call me Smithy, not Charles. Can't stand that my parents gave me such a poncy name. Now let's meet Kaden and get this interview underway." Smithy put his briefcase on the table and set out a notebook and pens, digital camcorder and a holstered sidearm.

Anna was fine with him appropriating the space as though it was his by divine right, but the sight of the weapon made the danger all too real. "Can you put your gun away before I bring Kaden in?"

Smithy looked at the gun and frowned. "Why?"

Jack met her gaze and nodded. "Because, if you're right and Kaden saw something—violent—happen, you don't want to spook him before you begin."

Smithy shrugged and dropped the holstered weapon into

the briefcase. "Happy now?"

If Kaden had the evidence Smithy hoped for, being happy was predicated on them living long enough to come out of this bizarre situation intact. Being happy was so far beyond how Anna was feeling; she chose to ignore the comment. "That will do for a start. Now, when you ask questions, please direct them to Kaden. He lip-reads, but I'll clarify where needed and translate his answers."

Without a backward glance, she left them and opened the door to the room Kaden had slept in. When he looked up, she managed a smile.

The agent is here. Ready to talk to him?

Yes. He followed her into the kitchen, pausing inside the doorway and eyeing Smithy with something south of enthusiasm.

Anna tried to see the agent as Kaden would. Taller than Jack, Smithy towered over all of them. His six-foot plus several inches frame made the tiny kitchen feel cramped. Did he use that height to impose his will on those he interviewed? Light blue eyes, glacier-blue in their lack of colour, shrewdly assessed his potential witness. Did he lack warmth and the ability to empathise? What if he pulled the 'bad cop' routine on Kaden? How would she handle that type of over-the-top testosterone?

With Kaden's best interests front and centre. Inserting herself between them she guided the teenager to a chair facing the agent. With gentle pressure on his shoulder, she got him to sit and took the place between them.

Jack sat across from her and set up Smithy's recorder, his smile encouraging, letting her know he was there for her and Kaden.

But will he side with us if the questioning gets intense, or will he side with his friend?

Smithy looked around the table and picked up a pen. "Everyone ready?"

With nods all around, Jack pressed the record button and

Smithy went through the process of identifying himself and having both Anna and Jack do the same. He outlined the process they would use to record Kaden's testimony and asked Anna to get the teenager to sign his name for the video.

Once the preliminaries had been covered, Smithy looked at the boy. His tone was surprisingly gentle, but his expression gave little away. "In your own words, tell us what you saw that led to you running away."

Kaden looked down at his hands for several moments. Then he lifted them onto the table, his hands slow at first, and then flying as he shared his story.

In the warehouse . . . wasn't supposed to be there . . . wanted to get uncle to let me go to coast with friends . . . they shot some man, blew his head to pieces . . . I was in the office and saw . . .

Kaden's face went pale.

Anna simultaneously translated, glad the recorder was capturing every word. Her mind went numb, went into autopilot mode. She couldn't think about what he'd seen, how he must have felt. Couldn't think about the violent story flying from Kaden's hands. Not yet.

Smithy met the boy's eyes. "So you saw your uncle murder a man in his warehouse in Brisbane?"

Three taps on his left hand.

"He says yes."

Smithy nodded and took some time, writing on the notepad in front of him. When he looked at the boy again, there was a hunger in the agent's gaze, in his body leaning forward; not desperate, but avid, almost willing the boy to give him the answer he craved.

Anna's stomach did a flip, certain Smithy considered what came next as crucial.

"What's the name of your uncle?"

Kaden spelled out *Ferdy Hickman.*

Victory, triumph, success. The spark flared in Smithy's gaze, warming the cool depths of his eyes. It left Anna cold.

"Did you know the man who was killed? Had you seen him before?"

A shake of the head. Kaden's throat bobbed as he swallowed and Anna's stomach lurched in empathy. His unembroidered account of the murder left her queasy.

Smithy reached into his briefcase and drew out a slim folder. "Ask him if he'd recognise the victim again?"

Kaden's eyes widened, and Anna glared at Smithy. "You don't mean to show him a police picture of the victim, do you?"

"Yes, one taken while he still had a face to recognise. Give me credit for some common sense, Ms Wilkins." He set an enlarged photo on the table and turned it to face Kaden. "Is that the man your uncle killed?"

Kaden picked up the photo and looked at it, nodded, tossed it on the table and raced into the bathroom. Sounds of retching filtered into the kitchen.

Anna stood, undecided whether to follow him. Her gaze fell on a second photo, one Smithy still held in his hand. One he hadn't deliberately shown, but which Kaden must have seen. A recognisable face no longer existed on the body. She slapped both hands over her mouth.

Jack stood and filled a glass with water from the kitchen tap and handed it to her. He wasn't green around the gills, not like Kaden before he'd rushed out, but as he filled a second glass, water slopped over his shirt. When he turned back to them, there was a look in his eyes Anna couldn't identify. If she had to guess, she'd say he'd made some decision he wasn't happy about.

"Looks like you've got your witness, Smithy. Let's take a break. Anna, can we make a pot of tea?"

"Tea? Of course—tea. I'll put the kettle on." The very mundancness of his request, of the act of making tea, grounded her. While she warmed the pot, found the tea leaves, set out four mugs, her brain whirled around the situation.

Kaden was the prime witness to a gangland murder. Worse, the murderer was his uncle, his only living relative according to Smithy. An orphan with no home. Until he was eighteen, he'd be a ward of the state. He'd be in hiding for the foreseeable future, always looking over his shoulder. How terrible to have no one. How unbelievably terrible.

Anna gripped the edge of the bench and swallowed back bile that threatened to erupt, even now, after the initial shock of Smithy's photos. The next step would be getting Kaden into witness protection while the police built their case.

And she had volunteered to go with him.

Chapter 8

Autumn winds stripped leaves from the trees and tumbled them around Jack's feet as he reached the fence marking the top of the paddock and the boundary of Anna's block. He shoved his hands into his pockets and turned his back on the easterly, narrowing his eyes as dust and dead leaves scurried past.

Guilt wracked him. He was responsible for what was about to happen to Anna. For the destruction of the safe life she'd slowly rebuilt here in Lark Creek.

The rational part of his brain knew the decision had been taken out of his control as soon as Smithy had his witness. Kaden had to go into witness protection and that was all there was to it. But Anna . . .

No matter how much Jack rationalised it, told himself he'd only prepared her for the possibility of what was coming, he knew. Manipulating her into a position where she felt she couldn't choose differently had been his choice. It made the situation easier for Smithy to have an interpreter with the teenager, someone with whom the boy had a clear, if tenuous connection.

Of course she had agreed.

But the moment he laid eyes on that second photo in Smithy's hand, his gut rebelled. The reality of Ferdy Hickman, the absolute certainty of death for anyone who crossed the king of Brisbane crime, accused Jack from every particle of the faceless man.

Jack's life thus far had been easy; work hard, gain an edge over the competition, do a little favour for one of the partners in the sure knowledge it would give his career a boost. In fact, taking on the practice in Lark Creek had felt more like a bonus. Aunty

Gloria certainly thought so when he'd called and asked her about the local rental market, and told her he'd be living in her town for several months. Now, the idea of doing favours sat like a brick in his gut.

Do a favour for Smithy by serving Anna up on a plate as Kaden's carer.

Disgust filled him. He'd put Anna in the path of a psycho with no thought for the still-fragile state of her mind. She could argue all she wanted, tell him she was strong and willing, but he'd seen her fear, her self-doubt. The silent *what-have-I-done* in her rigid posture when she looked at the photo of the victim—*post murder*—would taunt him when she left town. He felt the same self-doubt like a prickling in his neck, except his belonged in the category of what-*the-fuck*-have-I-done. In terms of monumental cock-ups, he took the prize.

As the wind dropped, he sensed he was no longer alone. Fearing Hickman had magically manifested on Anna's property, he turned quickly.

"G'day, mate." The gruff voice of Graham Muggeridge surprised him.

Jack corrected himself—Graham Peyton, same as Rick now father and son had found each other. "Hi Graham. Sorry, I was away with the pixies. What can I do for you?"

"Just checking Anna is okay." A soldier's bearing and a shrewd, all-seeing gaze had remained with Graham into middle age.

Jack met that gaze. "What makes you think she might not be?"

"Three males in her house. Sudden change of routine. She's been as predictable as Greenwich Mean Time–until today. Thought I'd call in on the way to see my son."

Jack had been equally as impressed with Rick's father as with Rick after helping to secure Rick's inheritance from his mother. A returned veteran, Graham had been in the Special

Forces. A combination of PTSD and claustrophobia meant he had chosen to live under canvas in the bush on O'Reilly's Ridge. What Graham didn't know about what happened in Lark Creek wasn't worth the knowing.

The ghost of an idea shimmered into being, elusive as autumn mist along the creek. "Good to know she has you keeping an eye out for her." He tried to catch hold of the idea, the potential for redemption.

"When I spotted you coming out of Anna's house I figured I was about to lose my job."

Jack frowned. "What?" The idea slipped through his grasping fingers.

"Thought you and she might have worked out you were a match." Graham let the implied question hang.

Jack's brain did backward somersaults with a twist as he tracked back through the maze of thought and conversation.

The idea? Where did Graham fit in that fleeting idea?

"How much of Anna's place can you see from up on the ridge?"

"Cottage, dam, driveway all the way down to the road. Mostly just this back corner that's hidden by the trees on *Dawnie*."

"Graham, will you give me your phone number? There may be trouble ahead, but I've an idea."

"For young Anna? What sort of trouble?" He blue-toothed the number to Jack before sliding his phone into a velcro-flapped pocket in his cargo pants.

"Bad. Let me get back to you, okay?"

"Son, if you don't get back to me pronto, expect me on your doorstep demanding answers. That girl in there—if she's in trouble and I can help, you let me know."

"Whatever happens in the next hour, trust me—I'll get back to you with some answers. Thanks." Jack strode down the slope towards the cottage, an unusual but strangely appealing idea coalescing in his mind.

***

"That's your idea? To hide in plain sight?" Anna shook her head.

Smithy said nothing, but his fingers worked overtime on the keyboard of his laptop.

Why wasn't the agent poo-poohing the idea, or was it so silly he chose not to grace it with a response? "We're talking about keeping Kaden alive, a state I'd also very much like to continue in for the next several decades, and your solution is to stay put? His uncle is a murderer who probably won't think twice about killing his own nephew to keep him quiet."

"No one in town knows he stayed with you. Nobody but Rory and the police have seen him yet. We openly meet him off a bus in Dalton and bring him here as your brother. What do you think?" Jack set his elbows on the table and watched her, his gaze keen, intense, willing her to agree.

Smithy sat back and closed his laptop. "It's unusual, I'll grant you that. To the point it just might be my preferred option."

"You can't be serious?" Anna pushed her chair from the table and eyed the two men. "You're telling me that the best option to hide Kaden is for him to become my younger brother and stay here with me, in this cottage where everyone in town knows I've been living *alone* for the past nine months and—and welcome back my supposed ex-lover into some cosy domestic bliss? Have I missed anything?"

Smithy headed for the sink and switched on the kettle. "Nope. That sums it up nicely. To outsiders, your former lover—Jack will make a great former lover, don't you think? He'll be living with you, having come to town to find you and win you back. I'm sure you two can come up with a reason why things soured between you and led to you dumping him. Your younger brother has joined you because blah, blah, blah. We'll work out those details shortly.

"If Graham Peyton agrees, he'll be your advance scout on

the ridge. He's got experience and the skills to keep you safe here. As an effective short-term solution, it's different and unexpected and it gets my vote."

"This is my life and my safety along with Kaden's. Do I get any say in things?"

"Of course. Might I remind you, though, that you agreed to stay with Kaden when he entered the protection programme, wherever that was to be. There was no statement that said protective accommodation would require a move." Smithy pinned her with a knowing look. "Is it the idea of staying here that worries you—out in the open—or is it having my honourable friend, Jack the legal eagle, hovering?"

Jack leaned against the edge of the sink, arms folded over his chest. Until that moment, Anna's main worry, her only worry, had been the idea they could hide where she was living in plain sight. It made no sense and now Smithy had put the image of Jack inside her house into her mind and her calm was totally shot.

"It's the whole damned thing spooking me. I'm already jumping at every sound outside. I've been used to my own company for too long to adjust easily to one, let alone two more bodies in my home."

Her gaze flicked over Jack and spiders shimmied in her stomach. Living under the same roof was a step too far. Yesterday, she'd granted him a measure of trust because he seemed to be trying to do the right thing by Kaden. Long hours of tension and focus had strained her *grin-and-bear-it* attitude, held together only for the sake of the teenager. But skirting around Jack twenty-four-seven? A shudder passed down her spine.

"Besides, how do you expect us to sell the people of Lark Creek on this silly story of Jack wanting to win me back?"

Chapter 9

Jack set his file on the coffee table as Anna came into the room. She looked through him as though an invisible wall separated them. He'd had enough. All evening she had avoided him and the discussion they had to have. It stopped here.

He stepped in front of her. "Anna—"

"Right, Mr Clever Dick, Smithy is in his swag out the back and there are two bedrooms here. One is Kaden's, the other is mine, and I don't share." Anna shoved a bundle of sheets, a doona and pillows into his arms. "Work out where you want to sleep and let me know in case I mistake you for an intruder in the night and clobber you."

Jack tossed the bedding onto the couch and caught her hand. She stiffened at his touch and her eyes widened with a haunted look. He let her hand go. "I'm sorry, but please don't go. We really need to talk, work out the details of our story if we're going to make this work."

"Your idea, you work it out." Arms folded across her chest, she tucked her chin down while looking up. Her eyebrows, several shades darker than her hair colour, emphasised the challenge in that *don't-mess-with-me* look.

"If our relationship had been real, we would have shared in its creation. Don't you think this will work much better if we do it together now?"

Her nostrils flared and she huffed a short, sharp, annoyed sigh, but she sat, perched on the edge of the far end of the sofa. "I can't believe I agreed to this."

"I'm sorry—"

"For goodness sake stop apologising. It's done, we're here, end of story." She sat back into the corner and drew her knees up, wrapping her arms around them and closing him out.

This wouldn't do. There had to be a way to connect with her; some common ground where they didn't look like what they were—two random strangers drawn together on an impossible quest to save a young man.

She was like a rose, so prickly he'd prick his fingers if he touched her. Resolved to draw her into conversation when she came into the room, now, in the face of her passive hostility, he faltered. She wasn't like other women. Discarding his planned opening, he looked up into a pair of clear hazel eyes . . . was she laughing at him?

"Oh, don't be a wuss. Faint heart never won fair maid. Tell me what you've got."

Mercurial. That was the word he'd been searching for. Anna's mood changes were like quicksilver. She'd keep any man on his toes.

"Just marshalling my thoughts. Okay. So—if we keep our story as close to the truth as possible, it will be easier to remember. Dates, events, places we've both been to. Twelve months ago I was working towards making partner in a big city firm in Brisbane. Mostly it was fourteen or fifteen-hour days, with not much time off for misbehaving. Where were you?"

"Twelve months ago—I was in Brisbane too, living out Forest Lake way not far from my parents' home. I worked as an accredited translator and did quite a few jobs for the state government. My last job was probably during the cyclone up north, or maybe the bushfire emergency. Sorry, I don't remember that period very well."

That period was late March. According to her file, provided courtesy of Smithy and which Jack had begun reading after dinner, the anniversary of the other home invasion was almost upon her.

Early April. No wonder she was antsy. Short of murder, it had been one of the worst home invasions he'd read about. Her parents attacked and tied up; her father undergoing months of rehabilitation. And she had walked in on the thieves. No wonder her memory of that time was random.

"We could have met a few weeks or months before that. How do you think it happened? Did we meet in a bar in the city?"

"I rarely went into the city, except when a job took me there. And I'm not a fan of bars."

"No bars. What about Tinderr or one of the dating apps?"

"You use them? Ugh, no. Too random. What about a party at a friend's house?"

That was more her style. He figured even before the home invasion, Anna would have preferred quieter gatherings. "A party is good. A fair majority of people meet their partners through mutual friends. Where and when was the party? New Year's Eve?"

"I guess it could have been. There are always tag-along extras that turn up at those parties. I have a friend, Tamara, who works in the city. She has an apartment in West End, on the fifth floor overlooking the river. I called in there around mid-evening. You could have tagged along with someone from your office."

"Okay, the friend of a friend scenario and plenty of party-hopping going on that night. We met at Tamara's New Year's Eve party. I kissed you at midnight in a corner of the balcony—"

"I wouldn't have kissed some random stranger, even if it was the New Year."

"I wouldn't have been a stranger by then. We would have talked and talked and I'd have been so charmed by you, and you with me, that that first kiss would have been inevitable."

"Such a cliché."

His lips twitched, but he held in the smile. She might not appreciate the idea he was beginning to enjoy creating the fiction of *them*. How they might have met—under better circumstances.

She didn't particularly like him, even though she had tolerated him for Kaden's sake.

That right there, putting up with him for a higher cause. A woman of strong convictions and a vibrant sense of social justice was exactly the sort of woman he would have been drawn to. He scoffed at his earlier stereotyping of her—blonde, quiet, standoffish. Of course she was his type—the type of woman he would have been determined to get to know better. Her refusal to kiss him just because everybody was doing it at the stroke of midnight intrigued him. That's why he had asked her out on a date. Just the two of them.

"You're right. Our romance was anything but a cliché. When would you have kissed me? After our first date when I took you out for dinner at the Italian restaurant at Southbank?"

"Nice first date but no. Not before the second."

"Why did you make me wait until then?"

"I wanted to see if you were going to stick around."

Naturally. Anna wasn't a one-night stand woman. He wondered if her choice was more about seeking deeper connection with a man. "Of course I was going to stick around. You had enchanted me and I respected your choices. Could I have enticed you into abseiling down the cliffs at Kangaroo Point?"

She gasped and her eyes widened. "Would you really drop your date over the edge of a cliff?"

"I'd be the one holding the rope and keeping you safe."

Anna tipped her head, silent as her gaze roamed his face. After several heartbeats, she nodded slowly. "I think you would. Okay, so you took me abseiling."

"And then I kissed you. You were so brave facing your fear of heights and so delighted by your first experience of being on the ropes that you flung your arms around me and kissed me."

"Which was it, Mr I-have-an-eye-for-detail lawyer? You kissed me or I kissed you?"

A laugh burst from him at that. "*Touché*. Which would you

like it to be?"

***

How would their first kiss have been? Would she have initiated it after the adrenaline rush of abseiling down the cliff? *If I'd even been able to let go at the top of the cliff.*

Distracted by his question about hypothetical kisses, and by the seductive quality of his voice, she almost missed the other part of his scene-building. "How did you know I don't like heights?"

Jack shrugged. "I didn't, but it fit with the story. You really don't like heights?"

She shook her head. "I'm not paranoid, but given the choice of crossing a log bridge over a rushing river or hiking a couple of kilometres to a ford, I'd do the extra legwork any day."

"I knew you were the sort of woman who'd go the extra mile."

A laugh huffed from her and she smiled. "Ah, I get it. Two kilometres—the extra mile. You're a real funny man."

He grinned as she recognised his pun. "That's one of the things you love about me: my sense of humour. I can make you smile even when you've been translating details of terrible disasters for hours on end. And then I hold you and kiss you until you forget the problems of the world and—"

"Don't overinflate your qualities."

"You mean to tell me you don't enjoy a man with a sense of humour?"

"I don't like comedians who are the only ones who think they're funny. Okay, where were we?"

"You were going to tell me who kissed whom on our second date. I'm kind of hoping you flung your arms around me and did the deed."

The more she tried to put off thinking about it, the more Jack's scenario took on a life of its own until the seed he'd planted blossomed and she saw herself rushing into his arms, pulling his head down and seeking his lips in a victory kiss. That's how it happened. Elation had lowered her guard and she kissed him on the second date.

She blinked as her lounge room came back into focus, and Jack—sitting there with his Cheshire cat grin like he belonged in her home. "Have it your way. I kissed you. So, moving right along, why did we break up?"

"Don't you want to cover the dates between our first kiss and our present reconciliation?"

"No." Exploring a pretend relationship with Jack felt too intimate, like it was taking on a life of its own. Already their first pretend kiss was replaying in her mind like an actual memory. She scratched an itch on her shoulder that felt like hives. *Great, her allergic reaction to stress had chosen tonight to make a comeback.*

"Nobody goes into that much detail. First date, first kiss, and they know all they care to know."

"Not quite all. How long before you stayed the night? When did we move in together?"

"Seriously, Jack? Is concocting a make-believe romance some weird turn on for you?"

He tapped his chest with his thumb. "You said it earlier. Stickler for detail, remember?"

"Okay. Then you tell me how long you think it took for me to fall into your bed. See how well you know me." Channelling her inner Lauren Bacall, she glared at him.

Jack leaned back and steepled his fingers. His eyes narrowed, studying her until the urge to squirm out of his assessing gaze almost overturned her control. "You resisted, citing the state of emergency with multiple bushfires and the likelihood you'd be called in at odd hours as your reason. The truth is, you weren't ready to commit to more than a casual relationship. I already knew I'd found the woman I wanted to spend my life with, a woman who values social justice and lives her life accordingly. Your commitment phobia and my pushing for more . . . That might be why you ran away to Lark Creek."

Her throat constricted, as though all the air had been sucked from the room. Her hand rose, settled on her throat. How could he know? How—after a bare two days in each other's company—had he sussed out that she'd run? As fast as she could out of Brisbane, ducking and weaving, not even leaving a forwarding address. Was she that transparent?

"We'll go with that. I'm going to bed. Goodnight." Wobbly legs barely supported her or, as undignified as it might be, she would have run out of the room.

"Tomorrow you can tell me how I found you again. Sleep well, Anna."

His voice followed her down the hall and into her bedroom. No use locking her door to lock him out. No use pulling the pillow over her head, or reciting the periodic table of elements. His voice became the audio as their romance played out in bright colours of summer against the backdrop of the Brisbane River, the cliffs of Kangaroo Point, the glittering fireworks of New Year's Eve.

"Damn you, Jack. Get out of my head." She rolled over and buried her groan in the pillow.

Undaunted, dream-lover Jack smiled the smile he gave only to her; the one that said he'd never let her go.

Somehow, in less than forty-eight hours, Jack Donaldson had done the unthinkable. He'd replaced the nightmare of the home invasion—the nightmare that played in her head every damned night, waking and sleeping—with their *romance*.

She wasn't sure which was more frightening.

Chapter 10

Jack stood beside Anna and raised his hand in farewell as Smithy and Kaden drove away from the cottage in the early dawn light. On the back seat, the boy pulled a blanket over his head before they reached the end of the driveway and disappeared from view. Even knowing the plan, convincing her to let the teenager out of her sight had taken the combined and not inconsiderable powers of persuasion of both Smithy and Jack.

"They'll be fine. It won't be long before we'll be picking Kaden up from the bus stop in Dalton. He'll be back in such a way that everyone knows *your little brother* is coming to stay."

Anna folded her arms around her waist, gazing down the driveway long after Smithy's car had disappeared from view. "Do you really think this is going to work?"

"Smithy is good at what he does. Better than good. Trust him, Anna; he's a top agent."

"But what if something happens and he needs to explain it to Kaden?"

"Kaden will lip-read, but you've already explained everything to him in detail. Things will go according to plan. Smithy simply won't accept anything less."

"But—"

Jack set his finger against Anna's lips. They were soft and pink, and her breath was warm on his skin. Surprised, she looked at him, her expressive hazel eyes wide and, for a moment, he thought about leaning down and kissing her lips. That's what newly reconciled couples did. They kissed and hugged, touched because they couldn't *not* touch. If Anna was worried, or sad, or hurting, he would wrap her in his arms and hold her until—

She blinked and, just in time, he remembered they were playing roles for the benefit of other people. There was no excuse to push her boundaries now. Not when they were alone.

Chastising himself for getting carried away in the moment, he turned towards the house. Flights of fancy weren't in his personality; facts and data and the realities of life were. "Come on. I'll help you clean up the kitchen, and then we've got groundwork to lay in town."

She followed him into the kitchen and was quiet while she stacked breakfast bowls and mugs and set them beside the draining board. As Jack filled the sink and added a squirt of detergent, she leaned against the cupboard beside him and leaned back on her arms. "Who do you think is the biggest gossip in Lark Creek?"

"No idea. I've been in town less than four months and spent most of that sorting out forty years worth of a muddle of files. I could ask Aunty Gloria if you like. Why?" He rinsed the mug he'd washed and set it on the drainer.

"Well, Smithy was keen for us to spread the news of our reconciliation around town as quickly as possible, before Kaden comes back. What better means than the local grapevine?"

"Ah, clever. How about we start with a visit to my aunt? She'll tell her friends at the CWA, and start the ball rolling."

"Okay." Anna picked up a tea towel and began to wipe the mugs as he set them on the drainer. "But don't go overboard embellishing the story."

He lifted a hand out of the suds, picked up the stack of dirty bowls and lowered them into the water. "One thing you need to know about me; I deal in facts. Embellishments I leave to the lawyers who present in court. And to creative people like you."

"I don't add anything that doesn't need to be there."

"Don't you?"

"No. Of course, our ideas of what is needed may differ. For instance—"

Before he knew what was happening, Anna scooped up a

handful of soap bubbles and set them on his head. "Now *that* is the finishing touch to this scene."

"Not quite." Quick as a flash he dropped a double handful of suds on Anna's head. She tried to duck and they settled on the side of her head and shoulder. "That's more like it."

Two sharp knocks sounded on the open back door.

They froze, each with a handful of bubbles, and turned as one.

"Morning. Hope I'm not interrupting anything." Rory Donovan stood in Anna's doorway wearing a huge grin. "I just wanted to stop by and make sure you were okay after the break in."

Anna flicked the suds off and wiped both hands on the tea towel. A flush of pink coloured her cheeks. "That's kind of you, Rory, but I'm fine."

"Yeah well, I can see that. Glad to see you've got company. Mum was worried you might have been feeling a bit on edge after—"

"No, all good." Jack seized the opportunity. "Actually, it might set your mother's mind at rest to know I'll be staying with Anna from now on."

Rory's amused gaze said he got the message. "Great to hear."

Jack set his hands on Anna's shoulders and kissed her temple. "We're really happy to be back together."

"I didn't know you knew each other."

Beneath Jack's palms Anna's muscles tensed, but she gave Rory a smile that would melt the hardest heart. "We dated in Brisbane about a year ago."

"A bit over a year, darling. Your friend's New Year's Eve party."

Anna nodded. "Tamara's party, yes. And then we split up and I headed out here."

"It took me a while to convince Anna to give us another go. We've been keeping a low profile, but after that theft, minor as it was, things changed and now we're back together." Personally, Jack couldn't imagine any man letting Anna slip through his fingers.

"Congrats. Reckon there's a few blokes around here will be disappointed at that news. Okay, gotta get back to help Dad with the harvesting. Later."

"Thanks for checking on me, Rory."

As soon as her neighbour was out of hearing, Jack gave her a one-armed hug and laughed. "Well done! That was easier than I expected."

"Easy?" The single word meshed disgust with disbelief. Her smile disappeared like clouds covering the sun. "Doesn't it worry you that we're lying to our friends, and to your family?"

Lying? He hadn't thought of it in those terms. Was it a lie when someone's life was at risk, or were there shades of grey that were acceptable under certain circumstances? But right now, Anna didn't need philosophical debate or legal argument on the fine line between lying and doing what was necessary. What she needed Jack could deliver in spades: reassurance.

"Rule number one: we aren't lying; we're playing roles in a real-life drama. It's easier if you let yourself sink into your part. Besides, tell me what part of this isn't true. We were both in Brisbane the New Year before last. Who knows, we might even have been at the same party. We did have a disagreement, and now we're sharing your house. All of that is true, even if the sequence is a little—fuzzy. The rest is just—"

"Embellishment?" One eyebrow rose, but she hadn't slapped him down.

He nodded. "Sure we've fudged the timeline a little, but if we play our roles well, we'll keep Kaden safe and, more importantly, we'll keep him alive."

She pressed her lips together, her gaze directed through the window. At last she nodded. "You're right. I have a tendency to overthink things sometimes. When we finish here, we can go for a stroll down the main street, and have coffee at the bakery. There should be a few people in town by this hour of morning. We'll give them a show of togetherness and hint at how you followed me here because you're besotted with me. Hmm, maybe I'll like being wooed and won."

"I'll do my best to make our relationship *memorable*, Anna. We might even decide we like one another along the way."

***

Gloria Bonnington lived not far from her great-nephew on the town end of Leonard Drive. As they climbed the front steps of the highset house and waited at the front door, Jack took hold of Anna's hand.

She hadn't willingly touched a man since the day of the home invasion and the feel of his hand enclosing hers sent anxiety, like raging battalions of wasps, flying in her stomach. Tremors ran through her body and she steeled herself not to pull away.

Back at her cottage, Jack had reassured her; what they were doing was reasonable and necessary, but her nerves had kicked in the moment his hand engulfed hers. His hand was real, like the man standing beside her. The warmth of his skin was real, not like standing in the wings waiting to go on stage on opening night. What they were setting in motion was make-believe, but Jack was so vibrant.

So male.

And they was about to slip into a role she would have to maintain for as long as it took to put Kaden's uncle behind bars.

That idea alone was daunting—one slip and lives would be at risk. But what was harder to contemplate was spending all that time under the same roof as Jack. The fact he was a lawyer had become less relevant as she watched him move mountains to create a good outcome for Kaden, but two days later, his constant presence in her home unnerved her, as did his ability to sound convincing about their *romance* when they both knew it was pretence.

Although . . . despite her apprehension about the role she was required to play, there was one unexpected positive in holding Jack's hand. He exuded a solid dependability, not the brash, testosterone-fuelled posturing of . . .

There was a click and a snick of a lock opening before Jack's great-aunt opened the door. Her gaze dropped to their joined hands and she smiled delightedly. "My dear Jack, and Anna! Welcome, come in. You're just in time for morning tea."

"Hi, Aunty. I hope you don't mind us dropping in unannounced."

"Not at all." She shuffled ahead of them along a dim hallway, leading the way into the warm dining room.

As they entered, Anna was aware of several people seated around the table, and a spread of cakes and fine bone china cups and plates. "I'm so sorry, we're interrupting your morning tea."

"Don't be silly, Anna dear. The more, the merrier. Sit down. I'll just bring out two more place settings."

Katy Leonard rose from her seat. "I'll get them for you, Gloria. Hello, Anna, Jack. Grab another chair from the corner."

Jack held the spare seat as Anna sank onto it, grateful the cloth-covered table would hide her more obvious nerves. Under its cover she gripped her hands together. "Thanks."

Jack's hands cupped her shoulders and he dropped a quick kiss onto her hair. "I'll be right back."

Heat raced up her neck and into her cheeks as she met uniformly curious glances around the table. Bessie Jenkins, Dora and Jillian Romney, Rhoda Alexopoulos, and two more ladies she thought looked familiar from a CWA fete she'd attended.

Bessie broke the silent anticipation, asking the question Jack had said would be on most people's lips. "Good to see you young people getting together. Where did you meet?"

Jack set a chair beside Anna's and slid into it. He reached for her hand and squeezed gently, before raising it to his lips in a slow kiss everyone at the table would see. "New Year before last we were at the same party; a friend of a friend in Brisbane. I saw Anna and was a goner."

"You never mentioned her to me, dear." Gloria looked a little bit miffed to have been left out of the loop. "And Anna's been in Lark Creek for what—several months, isn't it? Why ever didn't you tell me you knew my great-nephew?"

"I'm sorry, Gloria, but different surnames. I didn't realise you were related. And—well it was kind of a bad time for me." She glanced at Jack. *Your turn.*

He must have read her plea. "We dated for a few months and I was certain I'd found the woman of my dreams. Guess I got carried away—too keen to make it permanent. Anna left Brisbane and me and came west to Lark Creek."

Seamlessly, Anna picked up the narrative. "I needed time and space to think—clear my head. There'd been—*stuff*—happening in my family and I didn't have the energy to give to a new relationship."

Gloria leaned across and patted her free hand. "He always was an intense little fellow; even growing up, he was single-minded in pursuing goals."

Jack grinned at his aunt. "Is that a bad thing, Aunty?"

"Not ordinarily. But you scared her off, didn't you? I guess love blinds you to what's right in front of you sometimes."

"Or to what the other person needs from you. I knew that I wanted to be with Anna, but instead of giving her time to deal with other things that were going on in her life, I selfishly pushed for a commitment. In my defence I knew we were good together, and I thought I could be enough."

Anna's heart thumped as Jack spun their history. These wonderful women and Jack's aunt were buying into their story with gusto. "When Jack realised I meant what I said, he gave me time and then followed me to Lark Creek."

"I've had to be patient, which wasn't easy when the love of my life was so near. But I learned an important lesson; when you love someone, truly love them, sometimes you have to let them go before you can be together."

The collective sigh was audible. Everyone loved a good love story, and one that saw lovers parted and reunited was the best.

By the time they left Gloria's house, Jack was buzzing with confidence. He slid into the driver's seat and closed his door. "We couldn't have arranged to announce the news of our reconciliation any better. Aunty's morning tea was perfect."

"You were good, Jack. Really easy to follow."

"It helps sticking with things that are true, doesn't it? Our story hung together, and you were perfect in the role of newly-reconciled partner. A hint of shyness, and lots of loving looks my way."

She had glanced at him, but only to be sure she was on track. It had nothing to do with the light in his eyes as he revealed the course of true love didn't run smoothly. A light that made it easy for her to immerse herself in the story. A look that could seduce a woman into believing their pretence had real potential. It had resonated with every woman around Gloria's table.

"That was pretty convincing stuff you came up with."

He started the engine and made a U-turn before driving towards the main street. "What was?"

"About loving someone enough to let them go. You surprised me. I didn't think you had a romantic bone in your body."

Jack shrugged. "Silly stuff, but it did the trick. They fell for it because they wanted to believe in it. Tell people what they want to hear and they'll become complicit in accepting the fantasy. You even seemed to believe it." One eyebrow quirked up as he glanced her way and damn if the man didn't have the gall to grin.

Anna sucked in a breath. How close she'd been to forgetting Jack was a pragmatist. Jack wouldn't know love if it reared up and bit him. Remembering his laughing dismissal of women and love would be enough to keep her immune from his charm in future. It wouldn't do to forget again.

If she ever got over her anxiety about touching him.

She added a thick layer of sarcasm to her reply. "I won the prize for Drama at school. Sorry to burst your bubble—you *were* good and all—but I was just doing the job we set out to do. Good to know I haven't lost my touch, but don't get carried away in this roleplay. That's all it is."

His grin faded. "Good to know we're on the same page." There was an edge to his voice, the clipped response evidence that she'd put him in his place.

Keeping control was the key. Having him underfoot in her home when he wasn't at work was going to be a trial. So long as he kept his distance when they were alone, she'd make it through the coming weeks with her sanity intact. Moodily, she stared as leaves tumbled across the windscreen. If the fine days held, she could escape into the countryside and paint each weekend. Evenings would be more of a problem in the close confines of her cottage. "So, where to next?"

"That stroll you suggested along Main Street is enticing, especially after all the cake Aunty Gloria served. Want to take a walk with me?"

Keep it light and focused on the plan. Don't get sucked in by honeyed words and sexy smiles, or worrying about the next few weeks. "Sure. I can duck into the newsagent and order some art supplies. That will give us a reason to walk up to the far end of town, near the police station."

"And we can pick up some fruit and veggies for dinner if we wander back down this end of the street. I think we should discuss the celebratory dinner we're planning for tonight."

"What are we celebrating?"

"Progressing our story. Anna and Jack are back together."

"I'm not sure I can eat any more after Gloria's morning tea." Her stomach gurgled, drawing a laugh from Jack.

"Dinner is hours away." They drove in silence until Jack pulled into a space in front of the butcher shop halfway along Main Street. "What's your favourite meat?"

"Pork, preferably with lots of crackling."

"I'm more of a steak man, but I can live with that." He paused with his hand on the door handle.

She looked expectantly at him. "What is it?"

"Did you enjoy the Italian meal we had on our first date or do we need to adjust our story?"

"I love Italian, especially the zucchini flowers in batter. They're my favourite entrée at *our* restaurant."

"Good. Later, we need to sit down and share some of this basic stuff so we don't get caught out."

Her appetite completely disappeared. *One slip. That's all it would take to bring this crashing down on them.*

Chapter 11

While Jack stirred the gravy for their *reunion* dinner, Anna set the table with her best dinnerware. She'd been attentive while they'd been in town, holding his hand and hanging off his every word. As they strolled along the footpath, her smile had turned more than one male head in appreciation. In short, she'd played her part so well, he'd been in danger of forgetting it wasn't real. *They weren't real.* Not in the sense of an actual couple headed for—*God forbid*—the altar.

Problem was, she made it feel real when she clung to his arm and when her hip brushed against his thigh. Fixating on her lips and hips had been great for outward appearances, but her little smile, knowing and smug, had stung his male pride as they drove back to Cottage Farm. She knew precisely what she was doing to him. And he'd thought she was standoffish when they'd met at the police station!

He snorted and banged the wooden spoon on the rim of the saucepan.

"I didn't know making sauce could be so entertaining. Going to share the joke?" Anna brushed past him as she reached for the pepper mill, and then pulled back quickly. The brief touch of skin on skin reinforced the idea she was playing him.

This was payback. She was teasing him because he'd hustled her into this situation with Kaden.

He jerked his arm out of the danger zone and opened the oven door. "Idle thought, not worth mentioning." As if he'd let her know she distracted him simply by standing close.

The aroma of roasting pork and the delicious popping of crackling almost ready to come out of the oven drew his attention.

He slipped on an oven mitt and pulled the tray part-way out. "It's looking good."

He flicked a glance sideways and found himself looking into her eyes as she bent to look into the oven too. They bumped noses as they stood and she stepped back. Her eyes widened a little and a lick of pleasure flitted through his mind. That accidental touch had caught her off-guard and a flare of awareness—of him—had zapped in her eyes before she lowered them and put the table between them.

Two can play that game, Ms I-won-the-Drama-prize.

Anna gripped the chair, her gaze glancing past his. "I'll put the roast vegetables into a bowl if you'll carve the pork."

"Happy to. Do you prefer it sliced thick or thin?" He set the roasting pan on a trivet and reached for the carving knife and fork. So many little details flitted through that space where a relationship should exist; the types of things real couples knew about each other eluded them.

Thick or thin, for God's sake! So many ways they could slip up, give away the deception. When he'd suggested the plan, he'd thought it a good idea; maybe even a great idea. But every interaction he had with Anna highlighted how wrong he'd been.

"However it comes."

She busied herself hunting through the cupboard, and he was distracted all over again by the sway of her hips before she emerged with a serving tray for the meat and a jug for the gravy. Was his awareness of her part of the reason he'd pushed this plan?

Once they were seated and had served themselves, Jack picked up a piece of crackling and bit into it. "You were right about sprinkling the rind with salt. This is really good."

"Thanks. You mentioned we should learn a bit more about each other so we don't get caught out. How do you suggest we go about it? Random conversation or—"

Jack wiped his fingers on the paper serviette. "Why don't we proceed as though this is our first date?"

"We pretend we're on a date?" A quick frown scrunched her forehead while she cut a piece of roast carrot and popped it into her mouth.

"No pretence. This is our first proper meal together–alone. I wouldn't count the burger with Kaden and Marion as a date, or breakfast with Smithy, would you? Kind of puts a dampener on the romantic meaning of first dates."

"Fine. What music do you like?"

As he cut a piece of meat, he thought about the eclectic mixture of music he'd acquired over the years. "Hard to choose. I listen to some classical; lots from the sixties and seventies, especially musicians who were top guitarists, skip chunks of the eighties and nineties, then into the present century. What about you?"

"Ed Sheeran's music. I love the layers he builds up with that loop pedal, but when I paint, I prefer the sounds of nature."

"Understandable. No distractions. Does listening to nature help you sink into creating the painting?"

She stopped with her knife and fork frozen in the act of cutting a roast potato and looked at him properly for the first time all evening. Connecting gazes, seeing each other as a partner rather than a nuisance guest. Her eyes were darker than in daytime. Darker and more secretive, the pupils circled by a narrow band of honey-colour. Eyes that saw the world in a different way to him. "How did *you* guess that?"

The emphasis was slight, but he hadn't imagined it. *You— how did* you *guess that?*

Did she think he was so insensitive he'd missed her passion for her art, the way she became completely immersed in her work? Her dislike of him the night they met had been palpable. Maybe it had to do with some other lawyer who she'd had a run in with. But the idea she still thought of him, Jack, as incapable of empathising surprised him. It struck at the heart of who he was, how he saw himself.

"You claim I crept up on you when you were painting, but your wood floors make that nigh impossible so it follows you weren't *here* in that sense. I understand that about you. And when you talked about the transformative power of art, it was as though you had slipped into that scene. I understand you better than you think."

* * *

Jack had bent his gaze to his plate and, for the rest of the evening, Anna couldn't work out why there had been an undertone to his response. Questions forgotten, they'd finished dinner in silence. As soon as she set her cutlery in the middle of her plate, Jack was on his feet and clearing the table. He rinsed the plates, picked up his phone and disappeared through the back door, tossing a casual "Don't wait up" over his shoulder. The screen door banged behind him.

Unsettled by the frosty turn their *date* had taken, Anna sat on the couch and tucked her feet up under her. It niggled, distracting her from the novel she picked up. Realising she'd read the same paragraph several times and had no idea what it was about, she closed the book and let it drop on the coffee table. Why, when she was used to spending evenings alone, couldn't she now stop thinking about Jack and his moodiness?

She wandered into the kitchen and found herself staring into the pantry, unable to remember what she was looking for. If it was dessert, the pickings were sparse and it dawned on her that tomorrow night, she'd have two hungry men to cater for. Assuming Kaden had a typical teenage boy's appetite, she opened the shopping list app on her phone and added a number of items to buy before they met Kaden from the bus stop.

As she scrolled to the next heading and selected pork—her favourite meat—Jack's *I'm more of a steak man* ran through her head. Why should she change her buying habits just because he was staying in her home?

But snatches of the day's conversation flitted through her

mind. Jack had been agreeable about food choices, acceding to her preference in the butcher's shop. He'd grinned as he returned a plastic bag of Brussel sprouts to the display in the fruit and veggie shop when she'd said she hated them. *One day maybe I'll show you a way to cook them that will make you fall in love with them.*

All day he'd been pleasant, aside from acerbic comments about the women at his aunt's home wanting to believe in the fantasy of their love story. Why had that put her nose out of joint? It wasn't as if what he thought mattered to the roles they were playing. She couldn't think why else he'd put her back up, but she hadn't been herself. Maybe some of that annoyance had leached into her conversation.

So what if he was cynical about romance? He'd made the intrusion of two males into her house as painless as he could. She ticked the box next to steak and closed her phone.

Feeling restless, knowing sleep would be slow in coming, she picked up her sketchbook and a stick of charcoal and let her mind wander as her fingers flew across the page. When Jack returned from his walk, she would apologise for being snappy. Anything was preferable to the chill that had settled over them.

***

Out here, the stars hung bright, somehow closer to Earth than in the city. Jack lay back on the outcrop of rock and marvelled that he'd never noticed the difference before now. He wasn't sure he'd even glanced skywards in the weeks since he'd arrived in Lark Creek. He wasn't into camping like some of his mates, and evenings back in Brisbane, he'd either been working late or partying. Too busy either way to look up.

But in spite of the chill in the air, the urge to escape from the cottage had drawn him outside. Now, dwarfed by the immensity of the clear night sky, the millions of stars in the Milky Way, he accepted that he and Anna simply brushed one another up the wrong way. They could maintain the parts they'd been assigned in front of others, but in private, they were like flint and iron striking sparks off each other.

Of course, the situation didn't help. Nor the potential for disaster.

Neither did the layer of guilt he had brought on himself. He wasn't prone to beating himself up over things out of his control, but as he lay watching the stars, he felt his guilt like a physical weight lift from his chest and rise into the sky. Committed to the path he had chosen, he let it go with a sense of relief. The vastness of the sky would absorb it without noticing and he could concentrate on the fine detail needed to make this work.

There were sound reasons behind the choices he'd made, not all of them obvious. His kooky, adorable sister had often told him it was the universe pushing him in the direction he needed to go.

Universe or subconscious, from now on he'd go with the flow.

Turning his head, he saw lights still on in both kitchen and lounge room. Had he been oversensitive about Anna's comment? Probably. They were strangers struggling to appear intimate, trying to fit weeks or months of learning about each other into hours.

When he got back, he'd try to revive their abandoned conversation. He checked the time on his phone before setting it down beside him.

Soon. For now, he diverted himself with trying to pick out constellations, dimly remembered from science class.

Closing the back door quietly behind him, Jack stood still and listened. There was a welcoming quality to the silence of the cottage at odds with his earlier rushed escape. Presuming Anna had gone to bed and left all the lights on for him, he sighed. Delaying the discussion they needed to have until tomorrow was a frustration he could do without.

In the bathroom, he brushed his teeth hard and had a quick, cool shower, but the restless feeling wouldn't go.

He drank a glass of water and switched off the kitchen and

lounge room lights. Feeling his way in the darkness, he found the sofa and dropped his clothes over the back before feeling for the pile of bedding.

His hand landed on a curve of hip he recognised; that had distracted him on their walk through town each time Anna drew close. Soft breathing and a faint hint of her soap—*olive and thyme*—clinched it.

Why was she on his bed, asleep? Several scenarios ran through his mind, at least one of them X-rated. But the obvious and most likely answer was she'd arrived at the same conclusion as him. The need to share personal information transcended whatever differences were between them, but she'd fallen asleep waiting for him to return.

"Anna?" He spoke just loudly enough to wake her if she wasn't properly asleep.

Little reaction other than a snuffle and a whisper as her body pressed deeper into the sofa. As his eyes adjusted to the faint lessening of darkness in the room, he accepted she wasn't likely to wake any time soon.

Which left him with a problem. Her head was on *his* pillow, one hand clutching the end, and her body was cocooned in *his* doona. He could carry her to her room, sleep on the floor in his clothes, or . . .

He held in a soft chuckle as he headed down the hall to Anna's bedroom. She might not choose to share her bed, but he'd be damned if he slept on the floor while a soft, warm, queen-sized bed went begging.

##

Jack wasn't sure what woke him, only that some unfamiliar movement had dragged him from his sleep. He rolled onto his back and came instantly alert.

Olive and thyme and the familiar curve of hip beneath his hand . . .

Anna must have woken and made her way to her own bed. Half-asleep probably, she'd climbed in, too tired to realise he was there. Knowing he'd do the honourable thing, he lay still for several moments, listening to her regular breathing and cataloguing their choice of side in bed before he slipped quietly from her bed and returned to the sofa.

***

Sunlight woke Anna, streaming between curtains she'd forgotten to close. She flung an arm over her eyes and tried to recapture sleep and an odd dream already fading from her mind.

From the kitchen, the sound of the kettle whistling reminded her she wasn't alone. Not alone, and she hadn't offered an apology for—what was it she'd wanted to apologise for?

She sighed, recalling last night's dinner disaster. Why, whenever they were alone, did she and Jack butt heads? In their own ways, they were striving for the same outcome.

Footsteps sounded along the hallway, followed by two taps on her door, not so loud as to disturb her if she slept.

"Anna, are you awake?" *Jack*. His voice didn't sound as though there was an emergency so why . . .

Pushing herself into a sitting position, she pulled the doona higher before replying. "I'm decent. Come in."

The door swung open and a tray appeared, followed by Jack peering around the door. "Good, you're awake. I brought you toast and coffee. Thought we could continue our getting to know you session." His gaze slid to the other side of her bed before he set the tray on her bedside table.

A moment from her dream surfaced, imperfectly remembered, but she held back from glancing at the other side of her bed. *Only a dream, that's all it was.* She tugged the doona higher. "Thanks. Careful or I might expect this sort of service every morning."

"No trouble, if that's the sort of relationship you could see us having. Look, Anna, about last night, I'm sorry if I've come across as unfeeling. I know I got you into this, but—"

She raised a hand. "Stop right there. It's nice of you to take the blame but it's me who should apologise. Somewhere along the way yesterday, I crossed a line. I kind of lost the *off switch* to our playacting for a while and got miffed when you answered me honestly, which is stupid I know. Pathetic really, but I put it down to feeling out of my depth in all this. Anyway, I'm sorry."

He frowned. "Anna, you have nothing to be sorry for. I'm the reason you're involved as you are. We could have found a way around that document you signed."

"I know, or I guessed it wouldn't be binding. Not when circumstances changed so drastically. But I'm fine with it now. It makes sense to keep Kaden close. And just so you don't get the wrong idea, I don't expect or want you to continue with the charade when we're alone."

"We just have to get comfortable with switching in and out of our roles. It might take a bit of time, but we'll make it work. I believe that." He glanced at the tray and shoved his hands into his pockets. "So . . . mine is in the kitchen. I'll leave you to eat in peace."

"Sure, and thanks for breakfast in bed. One day you'll make some woman very—ah, forget I said that."

He grinned. "Come on out when you're ready and we'll talk."

As he pulled the door closed behind him, Anna couldn't resist glancing at the other side of the bed. The idea that Jack had been in her bed was ridiculous, part of a crazy, emotion-riddled dream. She *knew* it was a dream; knew, right up until her gaze fell on the imprint in the other pillow. She dropped the triangle of toast on the plate.

Broken promises, conniving schemer—her anger sat like a lump in her stomach, rose like lava in her throat. It burned so badly, angry tears pricked her eyes. Her trust in Jack, in his *honesty*, turned to ash.

She threw the bedding off and stormed into the kitchen. Ignoring the coffee that sloshed from his mug over her fingers as she slapped her hands on the table, she glared at Jack. "Care to tell me how and when and why you came to be in my bed?"

He closed the tablet he'd been reading, leisurely wiped his fingers on a paper serviette, and leaned back. The hint of a grin tugged his mouth up at one corner. "Sure I'll tell you how I came to be in your bed—*after* you tell me why you were in mine."

***

Fascinated, Jack watched her mouth open and close and open . . . she frowned, her eyes losing their intense focus on him, but no words came.

"Well? I could have woken you last night when I found you occupying my bed, and let righteous indignation boil out of me, but I thought I'd let us both get some sleep and then maybe today we could sit down like civilised human beings and talk."

Anna sank onto a chair like a deflating balloon. "I thought I dreamed—wait a minute. Were we in bed at the same time—at any time last night?"

"Yes—" He eyed her hands clenching, her shoulders stiffening as she reloaded, ready to blast him.

"Once I was conscious, I'd say I spent all of thirty seconds in bed with you before I did the gentlemanly thing and went to my sofa. I can't say how long you were in bed with me before your tossing and turning woke me. But I trust you behaved— *appropriately* while I was asleep."

"Are you trying to tell me that I—"

"Absolutely."

She covered her face with her hands and her voice was all muffled contrition and embarrassment. "Shoot me now."

"I'd rather not. You make such a fun pretend girlfriend."

She peeked through her fingers. "This isn't going to work, is it? We keep dancing around one another like a pair of boxers in the ring." Slowly she lowered her hands and spread them, palms down on the table.

"If by that you mean we're wary of each other, it's natural. You don't usually divulge that you prefer sleeping on the left side of the bed to someone you've just met."

"The pillow . . . I know I stay on my side of the bed all night, so I take it you sleep on the right or I'd have climbed in on top of you." Pink stained her cheeks and she closed her eyes for a moment.

"It's fine, Anna. Last night won't happen again." He didn't try to stop the cheeky comment dropping into the silence as he poured her a fresh mug of coffee. "Although if you ever decided to climb on top of me, I wouldn't complain."

Chapter 12

While Jack spent the morning in his office in town, rescheduling appointments and catching up on urgent work, Anna tidied the house and prepared a lasagne for dinner. When she was done, she walked through the silent rooms, expecting to feel annoyed about her impending loss of privacy as she waited for the invasion of males.

Plumping cushions and setting them on the sofa, her gaze landed on one of Jack's files sitting on a side table. A neat pile of bedding sat on a rug out of the way for the day, and there were other small reminders he'd inserted himself into her home and her life for the foreseeable future.

His presence was a nuisance, an annoyance, an inconvenience. So when, as two o'clock struck, she caught herself glancing through the window and listening for Jack's return, she added frustration to her mental list. *Frustration that he was capable of distracting her from her work and upsetting the precarious balance of her world.*

Within a short fifteen minutes of his return, five minutes after the time he'd said he'd be home, they were in his car on the way to Dalton.

"How was your morning?" Jack's attention was on the road as Lark Creek disappeared behind them.

Not so, Anna's. A subtle tang of fresh pine cologne wafted through the car, reminding her of her companion even when her gaze was firmly fixed on the passing scenery. "Fine."

Several heartbeats passed. An expectation of polite conversation weighed heavy in the silence.

She folded her arms across her chest and shifted a little

more towards the window. Couldn't the damned man take a hint?

"Did you paint this morning?"

A huff of irritation escaped. "No."

"Anna, have I done something to offend you?"

"No. I just don't feel like talking."

"Is that just with me, or is it this situation playing on your mind, because it sure is on mine."

"Of course it's on my mind—all the time." She turned and glared. "What a silly thing to ask . . ."

Jack glanced across at her and grinned. "Ha—got you to look at me. That's much better."

"Humph." But she relaxed her arms and one hand smoothed an imaginary crease in her dress.

"Seriously though, chatting about even mundane things can help take your mind off other stuff. So—let's start again. How was your day, Anna?"

Recalling her annoyance, her hand clenched in her lap. And then Jack's hand closed over hers and gave a gentle squeeze. "Let it go and think of the good things."

Let it go . . . good things . . .

She exhaled her next breath slowly, tamping down negative thoughts. The aroma that had filled the kitchen wafted from her hair when she looked at Jack. "I baked a lasagne for dinner, cleared space on the bathroom shelf and made more preliminary sketches for a series of paintings around Lark Creek. When I open my gallery I want to—" Her lips pressed together. Would there be an opening, or would Ferdy Hickman cancel out all their dreams of *when?*

Jack held her hand more firmly. "When you open your gallery you'll . . ."

"Do you think—" Her tongue flicked into the corner of her mouth. Why couldn't she let her fears go and focus on the other stuff, as Jack had said?

Even if the other stuff includes how irksome it is having

Jack in my home, it's better than giving Kaden's uncle power over how we live.

Jack glanced at her, his voice positive and reassuring. "It will happen once this is over. I know so. Tell me about your gallery. What will it be like?"

Closing her eyes, she visualised the empty building on Main Street, the elegant spire at odds with the boxy shape below. "The old church in town could be made into a decent art gallery with alcoves along each side and racks of directional lights."

"Great. What sort of art will you include? Only paintings?"

Drawn into sharing her dream, the drive to Dalton passed quickly as she described the business she hoped to build up. Before she knew it, they were in the supermarket with a trolley-load of groceries.

She paused and considered if frozen potato gems counted as a serving of vegetables.

"Anna, catch!" Jack tossed a packet of frozen fish. Instinctively she caught it. "Congratulations on catching tonight's dinner."

Giggles spilled from her.

Jack set one finger on her cheek. "You have a beautiful smile. Especially when you offer it freely."

Light as his touch was, it stole her next breath. The gesture smacked of the romantic when he'd been keeping things light-hearted. It put her on edge and reminded her they were playing a high-stakes game. She turned her head and his hand dropped from her cheek. "We need to get to the bus stop to meet Kaden."

Jack picked up a packet of frozen peas and tossed it behind his back. It landed on top of the meat. Nodding towards the nearly full trolley, he showed her the shopping list she'd shared to his phone. "Only a giant packet of popcorn to find and we're done with"— he checked the time —"ten minutes to go before your *brother* arrives. Easy."

He slung a casual arm around her shoulder as Janice

Lehman rounded the end of the aisle. She waved and pushed her trolley towards them. "Hello there. Nice to see you two together at last."

Anna had bet Jack it would take two days for the whole of Lark Creek to know they were together. He'd bet three days. "Who told you?"

"Katy shared your news last night at the meeting of the Lark Creek Tourism group. Oh dear, I hope I didn't speak out of turn, only I was delighted when I heard the news." Janice's gaze darted between them. "She only mentioned it because we asked where you were."

Jack pulled Anna a little closer. Not that she was going anywhere, but even in Dalton they had their roles to play. "Not at all, Ms Lehman. Anna and I want the whole world to be as happy as we are now we're back together. Great to see you but we're going to have to keep moving. Anna's younger brother is coming in on the bus and we don't want to be late, do we, darling?"

Anna made a show of looking at her watch and shook her head. "Oops, look at the time. Sorry I missed the meeting, Janice. I'll catch up with you later in the week if that's okay?"

Janice looked at Jack before nodding to Anna. "If I had a man like Jack waiting for me at home, chances are I wouldn't have made it to the meeting either. Enjoy your time with your brother."

As they pushed the trolley towards the check out, Jack leaned in. Warm breath tickled her ear and stirred strands that had escaped her messy bun. "We need to do something about this tendency of yours to blush when you're around me. Any thoughts?"

She disentangled herself from his arm and pulled her wallet out of her shoulder bag. "Paper bag, mask, or maybe I don't go out with you. Take your pick."

"I like your blushes. They mean I'm having an effect on you. And besides, *darling*, people think it's cute when they hear about our reconciliation." He unloaded the contents of the trolley onto the conveyor belt, and lifted the packed shopping bags into the trolley at the other end. As she went to pay, his hand closed over hers. "I've got this." He inserted his card in spite of her protests, and collected the docket.

As they walked back to the car, the need to assert her independence wouldn't be silenced. "I'll pay half. I just need to find an ATM."

"No need, Anna. Don't you know, you'll be paid for Kaden's share of food and board. That was me just paying my way." He glanced across the fields running behind the shopping centre as he opened the car door for her. A long distance coach was turning off the highway onto the connection road into Dalton. "There's the bus. Come on."

Quickly they finished stowing the shopping, jumped in the car and left the car park. Anna clenched her hands in her lap as Jack drove the short distance to the bus stop and parked. This was it. All their playacting before had been to set up this moment. From now on, they had to be on alert night and day. If Ferdy Hickman ever learned his nephew was in Anna's home in Lark Creek, there'd be nowhere to hide from him.

***

Jack eyed the teenager as he emerged from the bus into an awkward hug with Anna. Kaden's dirty-blond hair had been dyed just light enough that he could pass as Anna's brother, but there, the similarity ended. Where her eyes were hazel, Kaden's were blue and in profile, they looked nothing alike. But when they began a signed conversation, physical differences disappeared as they focused on one another.

When their gestures stopped, Jack stepped in, extended a hand and looked at the teenager. "Hi, Kaden. Good to have you with us."

Kaden's gaze dropped from his face and after a brief hesitation, the teenager shook his hand. He signed something and looked at Anna.

"He said he's glad to be here with us."

She signed and spoke, probably for Jack's benefit. "Where's your bag?"

Kaden pointed before grabbing a new-looking duffel bag as the driver set it on the footpath. He put both arms through the straps and hoisted it onto his back.

Jack folded his arms as he waited at her side. "I'm going to have to learn some basic signing you know. What if we want to have a private chat about his big sister, or a man-to-man talk?"

"I should have thought of that before. We'll start when we get home." Anna linked an arm through Kaden's and walked with him to the car.

The driver slammed the door of the baggage compartment and turned to Jack. "At least with that one you won't have any shouting matches. Quiet as they come, he was."

"Yeah. Good thing, right?"

The driver grinned. "Got three of my own. I tell you, a teen who *can't* talk as opposed to one who *won't* is a very different kid." He climbed back on board and within seconds, the bus slid away from the kerb.

Jack crossed the road and got into the driver's seat. "All set back there?"

Anna replied for her and Kaden. "We're fine back here. I'll give Kaden a refresher on key points and house rules while you drive."

"Good idea. Okay, home we go."

His gaze flicked up to the rear-view mirror more times than the drive home required. Anna's face was animated as she talked to the teenager, clear when she emphasised something.

She'd make a formidable older sister, he thought.

But once she'd finished drilling Kaden and turned her head to look through the window, her expression became wistful. Was she sad about the way her life had been turned on its head?

Jack made a silent promise that he'd do whatever he could

to help make things easier for her. To make them as good as they could be.

***

Home. Anna set three plates on the table and added a trivet for the tray of lasagne. It didn't feel like her place now she had two men living with her. She added a bowl of salad and cut several thick slices of crusty breadstick. Satisfied there was enough to fill two hungry males, she poked her head into the lounge room.

Jack sat in an armchair and Kaden was seated cross-legged on the sofa. He signed *hungry*. Jack copied the gesture and spoke the word. Kaden nodded. Jack repeated the gesture twice more before turning to Anna. He glanced at the boy before signing *hungry* to her.

Dinner's on the table. Come.

Kaden bounced to his feet and Jack grinned.

"I'm going to make a hopeful guess you said it's time to eat."

"You'd be correct. Lots of signed words are relatively easy to work out."

"Kaden's taught me five or six so far, and it's making me appreciate just how difficult it must be and how good you are simultaneously translating conversation." He followed her to the table where Kaden was finishing off a slice of bread. The teenager reached for the lasagne and slid a portion onto his plate.

"I grew up signing, but I believe it takes about six years and a lot of money to qualify as a translator. But it will be good if you can pick up a smattering of words while we're stuck here." She glanced up and bit her bottom lip. "Sorry, that came out rather rude."

Jack served a slice of lasagne onto her plate and then his. "It's true we're *stuck* here, but how we choose to deal with it, what use we make of the time, will make all the difference. Anna, I think we can make it pleasant if we try. There's no immediate danger, and we've laid the groundwork of our roles in town. How you choose to fill your days is still up to you. Our presence doesn't have to change that, not in any substantial way."

"You're crazy if you think things won't be different." She dug into the salad bowl and dumped a large serving of salad onto her plate. She set the salad servers back and pushed the bowl towards Jack. "But then again, it does mean I have two willing helpers to clean and cook and mow. Perhaps I was a bit hasty in my judgement."

"There you are then. That's looking on the bright side." Jack nodded before tucking into his meal.

"Definitely. And you know what—tomorrow I'm going to make up a roster of jobs. I think tomorrow will be your turn to cook."

Chapter 13

Jack and Kaden stood by the back door and window respectively, flapping tea towels at the smoke hanging like a pall in the kitchen.

"I think we buggered up this meal, mate." Jack spoke to the boy, unsure how much slang he understood. It was Jack's fault. He knew he shouldn't have left Kaden to look after the steaks while he took the call from Smithy, but Smithy never phoned just to chat. His news hung over Jack like the smoke pall in the kitchen.

"Ferdy Hickman disappeared as soon as the department began sniffing around his operation."

"Does that mean—"

"No need for you to worry yet," Smithy had said before ending the call. Debating whether to share the news with Anna, Jack had lingered outside until the stink of burning meat recalled him to the kitchen. By then the steaks were so well done they were beyond saving. Jack tossed the blackened scraps through the door, thankful Anna didn't have a smoke detector.

Anna's car appeared around the corner of the cottage before she turned into the single garage between the garden shed and wood shed. A moment later, she was walking towards the house, her frown growing the nearer she came.

There was no way to hide the stink or the smoke drifting through the window and door. Tea towel dangling, Jack held the doorframe and ducked his head out at the top of the steps. "It's not as bad as it smells."

Anna stopped and looked down at three charred, shrivelled pieces of meat that half an hour ago had been prime rib steaks. She toed one of them and looked at him. "Well that's good to hear.

And I suppose this isn't our dinner?"

"Okay, so things didn't quite go to plan but we can eat *al fresco* while the kitchen airs. Actually, we had a flyer at the office today that Rhoda and Leon have started up a takeaway three nights a week at their old café. Tonight's their opening night. Fancy some *souvlaki*?"

"That would be nice, thank you. I'll pour a wine and relax while you drive into town, shall I?" Anna raised an eyebrow and pinned him with a look that spoke volumes.

Maybe she was joking. *And maybe she wasn't.*

"Sure. It is my night to cook. Shall I take Kaden and leave you in peace for a while?"

"Whatever." She climbed the back steps and stopped, a hand over her mouth and nose before she waved it in front of her and sighed. "Everything's going to stink of burned meat for a week."

"Yeah, I know. I'm really sorry about that." Aware that his clothes and bedding were probably ripe with aroma of burnt meat, he sighed. "I closed the bedroom doors as quickly as I could. Reckon the worst of it is in the kitchen and lounge."

Kaden appeared at the back door with a glass and the bottle of red wine Jack had opened ready for dinner. He handed them to Anna and signed *sorry* and more words Jack didn't know. Maybe the teenager had accepted responsibility for his lack of attention.

Jack gave him a thumbs-up gesture and grabbed his wallet and keys. Signalling to Kaden to come with him, they left Anna to her wine.

It was late, nearly closing time as Jack pulled up in front of the Mykonos Café. His hopes for a quick trip sank as he looked at the number of people lined up waiting for their orders. By the time he and Kaden reached the register, Rhoda was shaking her head.

One hand rose, signalling for him to wait while she turned to her husband. "How many more serves you got left, Leon?"

"Might stretch to two. How many you want, Jack?"

"Anna's waiting at home for dinner and I was hoping for three, but I'll take whatever you've got left."

Rhoda eyed Kaden and smiled. "Growing boys need lots of food. Do you like baklava?"

Kaden blinked and looked to Jack for help. He signed *What?* and Jack was glad Anna had made sure he'd learned that word.

But he was stumped. How did one explain a foreign word like *baklava?*

He'd learned to sign some of the alphabet with Kaden when they started cooking dinner, but not enough to spell the word. Uncertainty drew a frown as he spread his hands and shrugged.

"I love it, but I don't think—" Kaden's name stuck in his throat, just in time. They'd been meant to come up with another name, as different as possible from the boy's real name. Something that wouldn't be connected to Kaden if the unthinkable happened and his uncle came to town asking questions.

Faced with supplying a name or raising suspicions and looking like a fool, Jack coughed, buying a moment or two while he raced through possibilities. "Sorry, Rhoda. I was trying to say we'd love some baklava, but I don't think Jed here has ever tasted it."

"Hello, Jed." Rhoda smiled, obviously waiting for his reply.

Jack smiled back at her and clapped an arm over Kaden's shoulders. "Jed's hearing-impaired and doesn't speak, but he can lip-read."

"Oh, poor boy. What's he doing in town?"

"He's Anna's brother, come to stay with us for a while."

Leon joined his wife and handed over two bags. "The last of the *souvlaki*. I put in some of Rhoda's *moussaka* too, for the boy. She made a big pot of it for our dinner—"

"We can't deprive you of your dinner, Leon."

Rhoda reached across the counter and patted his arm. "It's

fine, Jack. I made enough to feed an army."

Leon held out the second bag flat on his palm. "And this bag has *baklava* on a little tray. Keep it flat or you'll spill honey everywhere. You tell us how good it is next time you come in, hey?" The last comment he addressed to Kaden as he patted his belly.

Kaden nodded and signed *Thanks*, which Jack translated.

"Can you speak to him with that sign language?" Rhoda looked impressed.

Jack hastened to disabuse her. "A few words only. Anna is a translator. Both she and—Jed have been teaching me a bit. Reckon I've only reached toddler level though."

He nudged Kaden to move. "Thanks Rhoda, Leon. I'd better get this back to Anna before she thinks we've forgotten her."

***

Anna refilled her wine glass and sat back in a wonky camping chair she'd found in the garden shed and watched the flames lick along a dead branch. All through summer it had been too hot and dry to use the fire pit, but now the heat rolling off the flames fended off the cool night air. She tossed another small log onto the fire as Jack pulled into his parking spot behind the olive and wattle grove. Sparks flew up, brilliant orange against the dark blue sky of early evening.

Jack and Kaden strolled up to the fire pit and the teenager sat on a broad log, weathered to a silvery grey. Anna glanced up at Jack, gesturing with the hand that held her wine towards dinner. "I see the hunters have returned."

"Want to eat out here? That's a grand fire you've got going there. Be a shame to waste it."

"Sure. I got as far as getting the plates and cutlery out before the stink drove me out of the kitchen. They're on the table."

Jack set their dinner on the log beside Kaden. "Back in a minute."

Feeling mellow after a glass of wine, Anna called over her

shoulder. "I've got a second glass here if you want wine." She looked at Kaden, set her glass down beside her chair and signed. *Thirsty? Juice in fridge.*

He nodded and followed Jack inside. They returned together and Jack handed out plates and passed around the *souvlaki* and *moussaka.* "By the way, Rhoda tried chatting with Kaden. I had to introduce him, and—well, meet your little brother, Jed."

"Jed? Where did that come from?" Anna pulled out two skewers and set them on the plate on her lap. The name wasn't one she'd have chosen, but hunger diverted her attention from Jack's unusual choice. Rhoda's *souvlaki* had been one of the topics discussed at the catch-up meeting with Janice, and Anna was dying to find out if the school teacher's praise was justified. The aroma set her nose twitching. She pulled a small piece of lamb from the skewer, popped it into her mouth, and groaned. "I forgive you two for burning dinner. This is divine."

"A silver lining, maybe?"

"I'd call it 'lucky for you Rhoda's a wonderful cook'. I'm going to revise the cooking roster to include a weekly takeaway dinner. Now—why that name?"

Jack chewed and swallowed his mouthful before answering. "I realised too late that we hadn't discussed the details we'd make public about your family, but I was in a situation where I had to give Kaden a name. It was the first one that popped into my head."

"But—*Jed*?"

"As in Clampett. You know—'The Beverley Hillbillies'."

Anna shook her head. "Who are they?"

"You're pulling my leg. Don't tell me you've never watched it? It's an old television show from the sixties about—ah, I'll find it online and play it for you."

"Give me one good reason why you would think I'd have watched a fifty-year-old show?"

"Because it was funny and I used to love watching it when

I was a kid—"

Anna grinned, imagining a young Jack watching what would have been an old show even then. "How old were you?"

"Okay, maybe you have a point. But Kaden is now Jed, so can you please explain it to him?" He dug into his meal while Anna picked meat and vegetables off her skewer and Kaden demolished the *moussaka*.

Embers glowed and small flames licked the last of the wood by the time they rose to go inside. Kaden stacked the plates and headed into the cottage while Anna folded her chair and set it inside the screened veranda. She strolled back out to the fire pit. Jack had scrunched the paper bags into twists, which he tossed into the fire pit. They caught, hissed and flared briefly as grease and honey met flame.

Warm light danced over Jack as he bent and picked up the empty wine bottle and glasses. The leaping flames highlighted the planes of his cheeks and a determined-looking chin, square with a small cleft Anna hadn't taken much notice of before. What else had she missed in her efforts to maintain distance between them?

"That was a nice meal, thanks, Jack." Her voice held a softer note than she had used in earlier conversations with him. For all that he was a city lawyer, this business of getting to know him had lessened her dislike—of him if not of lawyers in general.

"You're welcome. I promise to try to avoid a repetition of the smoked meat in future though."

"How did you manage to burn dinner anyway?"

His jaw tightened and a muscle jumped in his cheek. Or was that a trick of the flickering firelight?

She wasn't sure. Not until he set the bottle and glasses down, and drew her down beside him on the log seat. His smile had disappeared at her question and he took her hand between both of his.

Anna's fears rushed back, tightening her stomach and clogging her throat. Her free hand rose to her neck. "Something's happened. What?"

"Nothing's happened. I had a call from Smithy that I thought I should take. No big deal. I left Kaden in charge of the steaks. He went off to the bathroom and forgot about dinner."

"No big deal? I saw the charred remains. Do you know how long it takes to burn meat to that degree?"

His thumb brushed her bare skin above their joined hands. His touch sent a shiver up her arm. Expecting the familiar anxious clenching of her stomach, she was surprised by a lick of pleasure at the contact.

"A while. Like I said, I got caught up on the phone."

Distracted by the new and disturbing reaction to Jack's touch, it took Anna a few moments before the oddity jelled in her mind.

"Jack, I've met Smithy. He doesn't strike me as a man who wastes time on idle chat." She watched his face with an artist's eye, the subtle shift and play of involuntary muscles. Was he deciding if, or how much to tell her?

Their gazes connected and he nodded. "You're right. Smithy doesn't do chatting like other people. But, Anna, it's really not a big deal and before I tell you what he said, I want you to know—we aren't in any danger."

"Now you're scaring me."

"Don't be. He called to keep us up to date. Kaden's uncle disappeared off their radar when the department started investigating him and his businesses. That doesn't mean he knows where his nephew is or that Kaden saw anything. Smithy actually made a point of telling me that. We're safe."

Her heart banged against her ribs like a hammer on xylophone keys, sharp, brittle notes zinging to the tips of her toes. Even two glasses of wine couldn't dull her sense of being caught in a trap. But she refused to let Jack see how much the news rattled her. Pressing her lips together, she sat up straight. "Okay, Smithy thinks we'll be fine. He's your friend, you trust him with your life.

I get that, but I'd feel a whole lot safer with some extra precautions in place."

"Like what?"

Until this moment, seeking her own form of protection hadn't occurred to Anna. But Smithy's news made the danger feel more real. She glanced at the dark bulk of O'Reilly's Ridge. Geilis Romney had shared a little of Rick's father's story and Anna knew that somewhere up there, Graham Peyton lived.

"He knows most of what goes on in Lark Creek by simply observing people." Geilis had shared that tidbit with a grin as their gazes connected.

Anna's thoughts ran to her dips in the dam during the hottest days of summer. Had Graham seen her summer swims? "How much can he see?"

"Part of Rory's property, your place, the winery—the main street of town, of course—around to Travis' farm."

If her cottage and land were visible from Graham's eyrie, maybe he'd be interested in keeping an eye on them.

"Graham Peyton—he's ex-army. I'd like to enlist his help somehow."

"What, like setting up security cameras around the property?" Jack nodded. "I like that idea."

"Cameras?" Continuous sight all around the property and advance warning of intruders sounded perfect. Secure.

"I'd only thought of keeping an eye out for strangers, but cameras . . ." Without knowing much about them, her vague idea crystallised into a concrete decision. She would learn whatever was needed and ask Graham for his assistance. "An extra set of eyes would be good. I'll ask him tomorrow."

Chapter 14

Graham Peyton positioned the last of the perimeter cameras in the low fork of a ghost gum overlooking the bottom corner of Cottage Farm before climbing down the ladder. "That's the last of them. Let's go back to the house and check the coverage on the monitors." He folded down the ladder and scuffed over the earth where the feet of the ladder had been until it was impossible to see where the ground had been disturbed.

"I really appreciate your help with all this, Graham." Anna looked up at the camera. Inconspicuous even when she was looking for it, knowing the tiny devices ringed her property made a huge difference to her sense of security. And she appreciated Graham's attention to detail, and the immediacy of his response to her phone call. "I can't believe you've got the system set up already."

"It's easy these days with wireless gear—just install, set a switch, and you're good to go." He slung a well-worn leather bag of tools over one shoulder and, slipping an arm through the middle opening, hitched the ladder over his other shoulder.

Anna collected the packaging and shoved it into a green rubbish bag. "I feel much safer knowing it's here, like eyes and ears around the property."

"Happy to help, but it would be more useful if I knew what problem I'm helping you with. You mentioned feeling safe. If you tell me what you're looking out for, I could tailor the system more to your needs."

Shifting the rubbish bag to her other hand, Anna glanced towards the cottage. "I—don't know how much I can share."

Graham's eyebrows scrunched together as he frowned.

"Are you in some sort of trouble, Anna?"

"No—not really. Hopefully nothing will come of it." Good grief, she was hopeless at keeping secrets. Her voice tailed away into guilt-laden silence. Was it reasonable to insist on secrecy when she had involved Graham without his knowledge; when she was going to ask him to keep watch over them from the ridge?

Smithy's final words weighed on her. *Tell no one.*

"I'm sorry, Graham. It's not really my secret." If only she'd thought through how to answer the question, but her evasiveness now had alerted Graham that trouble was brewing. His piercing gaze, so like his son's, stripped away her layers of defence. She took a few steps towards the cottage and stopped when she realised he wasn't following.

"Secrets, is it?" He tapped the handle of an electrical screwdriver on his thigh and glanced up at the camera before slipping the screwdriver into his tool bag. "How about I tell you what I think?"

Anna shrugged. She couldn't stop him from speculating, but not in his wildest dreams would he come close to working out what was going on. "Give me your best guess, but I don't expect you'll get it. And even if you do—what's that phrase they use on American dramas? I know—I can neither confirm nor deny."

They strolled side by side up the slope, weaving between patches of bushes and low trees her landlords had allowed to grow on the lower corner to create more privacy for the cottage when the land was no longer part of the main farm. That element of privacy had appealed when she moved in. Now, she imagined Hickman's gang using the bushes for cover as they sneaked up on the cottage. *Graham's cameras will spot them. First line of defence.* Pushing back against dark thoughts, she prompted Graham. His suspicions would ease her lurid imaginings. "So tell me what you think."

"Fair enough. First, you suddenly have Jack Donaldson staying with you and the talk in town is that you're lovers who fell out and have now reconciled. That's bulldust. I'm pretty sure you hadn't met before the young fellow got arrested. My guess is that's what brought you two together in the first place."

Anna sucked in a breath, but kept walking, her gaze firmly fixed on the cottage. "Go on."

"That young fellow most folks in town are saying is your little brother, he looks nothing like you. It's the boy Rory penned into his chook house and he's sporting a half-arsed dye job."

Hands in a grip that tightened with each correct guess Graham made, Anna kept walking. If he knew, if it was that obvious to a man who lived his life at a distance from everyone, how could they hope to fool others in town? Or Kaden's uncle if he showed up?

"No comment, Anna? Okay, the final piece. Your visitor the other day, the tall bloke in a rental car that was too small for him—even from up on the ridge I could tell he wasn't your friend. I'd say Jack knows him and that he's a police officer. They have a certain look, a way of moving, and he was on alert. Whatever is going on has to do with that young bloke. The boy looked to me like he was cornered. How am I doing so far?"

Shock, surprise, trepidation—they brought Anna to a standstill. She stared at Graham. "You got all that by just watching us from up there?"

He nodded once. "You can learn a mighty lot by observing people and their comings and goings. So, are you worried the boy will try to run, or are you protecting him from someone? I suspect the latter."

How could she tell Graham he was spot on when Smithy had stressed the importance of not telling anyone the truth? "Graham, I—"

"It's okay, lass. Your reaction was answer enough."

"I'm sorry. If I could tell you . . ." She shrugged again. "Should I be worried our plan isn't good enough or happy you're so amazingly good at observation?"

He chuckled and rubbed a thumb along his bristled jaw.

"Seems to me most folks are happy for you and Jack. I'd build on that. And let the boy out of the house. Keeping him hidden might look suspicious."

"You know, I thought I had a good eye for detail. You're much further away and yet you see so much more."

"Call it the long view. And it helps when you're not worried someone's out to get you. Come up to the ridge one day and I'll show you this land like you've never seen it before. It's beautiful when you're looking out over the valley. Reckon you might like to paint it." There was a tone in his voice that revealed how much he loved the ridge where he lived.

"Thanks. I'd like that. Would you like a tea or coffee before you check the monitors? I'll introduce Ka—Jed too."

"Ka-jed! Hmm, better practise that before you take him into town again."

"You're right. I will. And just so you know, *Jed* is hearing-impaired. Unlike many others, he doesn't speak."

"He signs? No problem. And yes to that coffee."

Anna led the way inside and put the kettle on to boil. From the lounge room, she could hear the clash of metal, sword on sword, and pings indicating Kaden was playing a computer game on the tablet she'd let him use. She set out coffee mugs before taking Graham through.

Kaden was sprawled on the sofa. As her shadow crossed the screen he paused the game and looked up.

She signed, *I have a friend to introduce.*

Graham stood beside her and signed his name before holding out his hand. Kaden stood and shook it.

Anna tipped her head. "Why didn't you tell me you could sign?"

"I can't. Well, only a few words and phrases." He added a slow and simple invitation for Kaden to climb the ridge.

Kaden replied with fast signing and looked expectantly at him.

Graham turned to Anna. "That's just about exhausted what I know. What did he say?"

"That he'd love to visit you and will you show him the types of trees growing up there." She asked Kaden, *Why trees and not the view?* and then interpreted his answer for Graham. "I think Jed is interested in the different woods. Seems he likes working with wood."

"Interesting. Could be a way to get him out of the house. Bring him when you come, or send him up the track alone if you need some down time and I'll meet him where it gets steep. Most folks don't go beyond that point."

"Thanks, that's kind of you, and it might be a way to keep him occupied while we wait for—things to get sorted out." She had to be more mindful of what she said. Graham knew most of the situation—unofficially—but that didn't lessen the need for her to guard her words.

"Maybe Gei and Rick could use another hand in the vineyard a couple of days a week. If the boy likes working with wood, Rick was talking about extending the display area in the cellar door."

"Thanks, I'll ask Jed and then talk to Gei and Rick. Now, that coffee won't make itself." If Graham's kindness caused her eyes to prickle with unshed tears, then she'd bottled up her fears and worries to an unhealthy degree.

"I'll check the monitors if you want to bring the coffee through." Graham took Kaden with him into her bedroom where she soon joined them. They looked comfortable together in front of two split screens showing the view along her fence lines. Graham had also set up cameras at each corner of the house. Nobody could approach undetected. As an added precaution, he'd suggested leaving the gate at the bottom of the driveway closed. "That will allow you time to check out who's in any car that approaches. I've wired the gate so when someone opens it, you'll hear a beeping when you aren't in your bedroom. If you don't like the look of your visitors, it gives you time to scoot through the fence to your neighbours or head up the track to the ridge."

Anna studied the angle and line of sight. The camera on the lower corner of the property showed a clear view of the gate, the road—and one of the dairy farm's cows contentedly munching grass at the side of the road. "I'd better ring the Hamiltons and let them know they have an escapee." Peering closer at the calf, she grinned. "I'm pretty sure that's Hughie."

"Hughie, as in the grass-is-always-greener Hughie?" Graham chuckled before drinking his coffee. He set the cup down and panned the camera across the view as he spoke. "Funniest thing I saw was Gei trying to keep that calf on his side of the fence and out of her vines. He manages to escape pretty regularly. Now, see how you can change the angle of this camera? The others are fixed, but this one moves. You'll need to change the battery if your—situation continues for a few months."

"I can only hope it's resolved quickly. This looks wonderful, Graham, thanks so much."

"You're welcome. Can you explain to Jed that I'll be back with a special light for the lounge room that will flash when someone opens the gate? Because he can't hear the warning beeps he needs the visual cue. I'll need to pick up a couple of items to make it work, but that way, he'll have warning of visitors approaching."

He finished his coffee, stood and stretched. "From now on, this is your HQ, your headquarters. One of you needs to run daily checks of all the cameras, and test the movement of the one at the front gate. I'll move camp to a better command position. It will be higher, but I'll have you in my sights throughout the day."

Thanking her lucky stars for Graham, Anna signed to Kaden what Graham had just explained.

She'd met Rick's father only the once, at the vineyard harvest party, and yet he'd immediately come to help when she'd rung him. His willingness to help was above and beyond anything she'd expected and his competence and attention to detail made her feel as though they had a better than fifty-fifty chance of escape if the unthinkable happened. "How can I thank you for all you've done?"

"Stay alert and you'll stay safe. I'll be on my way." He signed *Goodbye* to Kaden and left by the back door.

Anna watched him disappear into the trees between her property and the Donovan place. Tracing the path he would follow, try as she might, she couldn't catch another glimpse of him. Rick had been right about his father's mad tracking and camouflage skills.

She wandered back into the house and picked up her sketchpad. In the midst of the second biggest upheaval of her life, the urge to create surprised her.

Was it because Graham's work had bolstered her sense of security?

Chapter 15

Jack sat in front of the monitors and whistled. "Graham is good. I don't think there's one millimetre of boundary not covered by his cameras."

"I know. And the funny thing is I did some painting for the first time in days. It was like my mind was free to focus on the canvas because I didn't feel I was looking over my shoulder all the time."

Jack turned sideways on the chair. As Anna tucked a strand of hair behind her ear, he saw her left hand was streaked with blue paint the colour of distant hills. The sight of that paint streak made him happy for her. "That's great. Is it a scene for your gallery?"

"It's the view across to Thornyhill. I may include it in my first showing—if I can convince the owner of the church to lease the building to me."

"I could negotiate with him on your behalf if you like."

"Her. The owner is a woman and so far, she hasn't been interested in talking to me, but I won't give up. Not now."

"What's changed that has firmed your resolve?"

She picked up a pencil and began drawing on a notepad as she worked her way through to an answer. "I feel like I've been drifting through my life for the past year. It's strange, but this situation we've found ourselves in has brought things into perspective. Now, I find myself wanting to achieve certain goals and that means getting through the next however long."

"Sounds like you've found your reason to live."

"Fearing for my life, even when the threat is as distant and elusive as Hickman, has sharpened my focus on what's important. The gallery is what I want. When this is all over, I'll find the owner of the building and convince her to lease it to me."

"It's good to see you more relaxed. The day we met you were so tense I thought you'd snap under the strain."

"I'm not that fragile, Jack."

"I've learned that about you. You're resilient and brave, and I admire how you've accepted the challenges of caring for Kaden. I guess I underestimated the shock you'd just had."

"Shock?"

"Kaden breaking into your home."

Her pencil stilled on the page as she glanced at the small corkboard beside the monitor and frowned. A calendar sat amidst photos of what he assumed were her family. The likeness to her mother was clear, but she had a way of tilting her head that angled her chin the same as her father. "I have been—tense for a while."

"Was it learning that Ferdy Hickman had disappeared when Smithy's investigation got underway that worried you, or was it something else?"

He watched Anna's gaze flicker away. If only he could wipe out all the worry associated with keeping Kaden safe and make Anna feel secure in her own home again, he would. But she had more layers than an onion. He peeled one back only to find another.

"That was part of it. Tomorrow is the first anniversary of the break-in."

He followed the direction of her gaze. Tomorrow's date was circled in red felt-tip pen. Smudges of red marked the area below, as though a hand had grabbed the anger and sadness of that day and scattered it over the rest of her life like a branding iron. He supposed, in a way, it had. "Your parents were injured in that attack. I can see how that would make you feel tense, but—what do you feel now, Anna?" He was no psychologist but he could see Anna teetering on the edge of confronting what had happened a year ago. The danger to Kaden and, by extension, to her had brought more than her goals into focus.

"Anxious. The date is like a huge neon sign flashing closer and closer, growing bigger with each day I cross off the calendar. I feel like it's so big it's going to steamroll right over me. But at the same time worrying about whether Hickman might find us has taken over some of that real estate in my mind. I can dwell on the past, or I can focus on doing all I can to ensure Kaden has a future."

Jack tightened his grip on the back of the chair. If he didn't hold on, he'd do something totally inappropriate, like pulling Anna into his arms and making promises he'd keep her safe, and help to keep Kaden safe. She'd hate that, not just because she valued her independence, but also because he had no right to hold her. Not when they were alone; not when the audience for whom they played the role of reconciled lovers was absent.

At this moment, he wished he had that right. "Can you think of anything that would make tomorrow easier? Do you want to talk to your parents?"

She shook her head and added a few lines to her sketch on the notepad. "I don't have my new phone set up for speech to text, but I'll message them."

"Do you think—"

"Can we not talk about this any more? I'd rather try to focus on positives. Graham's security set up feels like one small positive in days of negatives." She turned deliberately to the monitors.

Jack got the message. He didn't agree with bottling up worries as Anna had been doing, but her choices were her business. Glancing at the notepad now her hands weren't covering the page, he saw she'd drawn a bird flying out of the open door of a cage. It was headed for the sky.

Anna scrolled through each camera view, finally coming back to the front gate. She manipulated the camera and looked both ways along the road. "Looks like the Hamiltons have managed to keep Hughie on their side of the fence."

Did Anna have a problem, or was he seeing one where none existed? Glancing at the bird sketch, he shook his head. Being here to help had felt right when he'd made the offer, but maybe it had more to do with his guilty conscience than Anna needing him hovering around her like some overprotective mother hen.

"It looks like all's quiet on the eastern and western fronts. Would you like a glass of wine or a beer with dinner? I picked up both from the bottle shop on the way home."

"What's for dinner?"

"I've got the makings of a chicken laksa. The easy version. Beer?"

"Maybe white wine. Thanks. Do you want a hand with cooking?"

"No. You relax. Kaden's going to help me. If nothing else, he's learning some new skills while he's with us."

"Speaking of which, Kaden asked Graham to show him the trees on the ridge. I learned today that he's interested in building things and Graham suggested Rick might take Kaden on to help install some new display cabinets for the cellar door. What do you think about letting him out like that?"

"I'll run it by Smithy. Personally, I reckon it sounds a good idea. The boy will go stir-crazy if he's stuck here all the time. I'll try phoning while dinner's cooking. If Smithy gives the go-ahead, we can ask Rick about the possibility tomorrow."

"That would be wonderful. Maybe we can pick up a few basic tools for Kaden next time we're in Dalton?" Anna's smile was like sunshine on a winter's day, sudden and warm and it knocked him for a six. She rarely smiled. Scratch that. She hadn't smiled *at him* like that since they'd met. Turning the full force of her smile on him had done something crazy to his brain. Addled it, or maybe short wired it.

He couldn't remember a word she'd just said. "Whatever you think."

"You're very agreeable tonight."

"I feel as though things are starting to work out very nicely." He grinned and left the room. A moment later, he popped his head around the door. "Do you want that wine now or with dinner?"

"I'll wait and have mine with you. I just want to message Mum and Dad."

"Okay. I'll call you when dinner's on the table."

Kaden had finished chopping the chicken breast when Jack returned to the kitchen and the quick version of laksa meant opening a bottle of sauce and a tin of coconut milk and stirring it all together.

As he stirred the mixture, he ran Graham's idea past Smithy. "Rick is Graham's son. I feel confident he'd be suitable for a test run with Kaden. And the winery is just down the road from Anna's place. Location wise, it's close while giving Kaden a bit of breathing space."

"He's got a good point, your army guy. Yes, let the boy be seen out and about, but be sure to mention that he's Anna's brother every now and then. Keep it simple, and keep it vague."

At the other end of the line, Jack could hear sirens wailing and Smithy ended the call with the information he'd be out to check on them within a couple of weeks. "Don't do anything I wouldn't do, mate."

"Like what? There's so many to choose from."

Smithy snorted. "Anna's an attractive woman, but remember, this situation is fake. Don't lose your head, mate." The line went dead.

Jack stared at his phone as though it might bite him. *Fall for Anna? Did Smithy really think he was in danger of falling for her?* Just because he'd thought about hugging her didn't mean he wanted a relationship with her. Smithy was cracked in the head if he thought that.

By the time he'd ladled laksa over the noodles in three

bowls and Kaden had set the table, Jack had shuffled off the odd feeling Smithy's comment had drawn from him. Anna's painting of the view to Thornyhill Farm sat on an easel in the corner of the kitchen. There was a lighter touch to the colour and composition, embodying the positivity Anna had mentioned. It sat in the house like . . . He glanced up searching for a simile to suit the feeling.

Smoke stains on the walls and ceilings dampened his good mood. The last time he and Kaden had attempted to cook, Smithy's phone call had blasted his peace of mind, the meal and Anna's sense of security to smithereens.

Anna entered, catching him holding the saucepan and ladle and glaring at the evidence of his last culinary failure. He met her gaze and nodded at the offending surfaces. "I'll climb up and wash the walls and ceiling on the weekend."

"I'll help you. It's not all from your *well-cooked* steaks. The walls weren't exactly pristine when I moved in." She gave a half-smile that was more like a twitch of the lips as she sat in her place at the table. The joyful smile she'd given him had vanished and she seemed weighed down by whatever had passed between her and her parents. She smiled and chatted with Kaden, but her preoccupation during dinner was clear.

"How are your parents?"

Anna moved her fork around in her bowl without picking up any food. "Mum has locked them inside the house and closed the curtains."

"Because of the date?"

Anna shook her head. "Not just the date, although that hasn't helped matters. Every day since the attack as soon as the sun goes down, she locks them inside. Dad said he can't entice her into the garden for more than a few minutes in the middle of the day because she gets fidgety and keeps looking over her shoulder. It's awful."

"That's pretty tough. Did your parents see anyone after the event—a therapist or counsellor?" There were times when Jack wondered if Anna had spoken to anyone about the attack. She seemed to need closure, but it wasn't his business to say so.

Kaden had been watching their conversation in silence for several minutes, but now he tapped the table to get their attention. *What happened?*

***

Startled, Anna looked at Kaden. She'd forgotten his presence as she mulled over the conversation with Dad. Her father's messages had shattered the tiny slice of optimism that had replaced her anxiety after Graham's departure. She set her fork down and dabbed her mouth on a paper serviette, buying time before she answered him.

My parents were injured in a home invasion a year ago. Tomorrow's the anniversary. I'm feeling a bit . . .

What?

Nothing. It's just a date on the calendar.

Did I make it worse when I took your muffins?

She could lie and absolve him of that guilt, if that's what the look on his face was. Would that help him in the long run? But Kaden had so much more to deal with. Her anxiety was about unresolved issues; his—could be his life. *Not worse, just a reminder to lock my doors. Finished with your plate?*

He scrutinised her face, probably unconvinced if his narrowed eyes were anything to go by, so she smiled. *I'm fine.* He nodded and carried his plate to the sink where he rinsed it.

She was aware of Jack's intent appraisal before he bent his head over his bowl and finished his meal. Grateful he'd let the conversation drop, she took a small bite of chicken, but her stomach rebelled against the food.

Jack stood, lifting his empty bowl and glanced into her still nearly full one. "Not hungry, or not to your taste?"

She looked up. "It's delicious, but I'm not very hungry. I'll put it in the fridge and maybe eat it later." Her chair scraped as she pushed it back, the screech sending goose bumps traipsing down her spine.

When she'd covered her bowl with cling wrap and set it on a shelf in the fridge, she glanced at Jack. He was frowning and she had an awful feeling he was going to pursue the reason for her loss of appetite. Having learned how he liked to talk things through—not feelings, but anything he perceived as a problem—she spoke before he could. "I'm tired. I'm going to bed. Goodnight."

Letting him show he cared for her in any way would undermine her resolve to be strong. She hated feeling vulnerable, hated it with a passion.

She raced through her bedtime routine and closed her bedroom door. But she couldn't shut out the knowledge that Jack was worried about her. Caring meant connection, and connecting with Jack was fraught. The last thing she wanted with Jack was a real relationship. What was the use of feeling something for him when this was all pretend? Their time together had a use by date and it was linked to the jailing of a gangster. Once the gates of the jail shut on Ferdy Hickman, Jack would be out of her life and back to Brisbane, cosy in his corner partner's office.

She refused to let him into her life any further. The hole when he left would be impossible to fill.

Chapter 16

Jack rested his head on his bent arm and stared through the gap in the curtains. The dark night outside was barely lighter than the lounge room in which he lay, frustrated as sleep eluded him. Somewhere in the distance a mournful bird sent its cry into the dark sky. The sound skittered through his mind like an ill omen.

"Bah, no such thing as omens." Speaking the words into the silence of the room, he pushed away the nagging fears Anna's strange mood had brought to the surface and contemplated getting up and working on a file. If he got up, he could work in the kitchen so no light leaked under the bedroom door and disturbed Anna. Maybe he'd make a warm milk drink.

Except he disliked milky drinks. Maybe he'd try one of the herbal teas Anna preferred before bed and—

A scream broke the silence. Loud, angry—frightened.

"Anna!"

He threw off the covers and raced to her bedroom. Flinging the door wide, he crouched, ready to tackle an intruder.

The soft glow from the monitors on night mode fell across Anna. Alone in her room she writhed in a tangled mess of sheets, her head tossing from side to side on her pillow.

"Leave him alone, leave him . . ." Her hands reached out, groping blindly as though she fought off an imaginary attacker. Or defended someone.

Jack couldn't tell which. He sat on the edge of the bed, took hold of her hands and spoke her name gently. "You're okay, Anna. No one's here to hurt you."

As her frantic struggle ceased, he waited for her to open her eyes. He took hold of her shoulders and gave her a gentle shake.

"Anna? Do you want me to put the lights on?"

Her eyes remained closed, but she shook her head. Then she whispered something his fevered brain interpreted as 'Hold me.' She'd never ask that, not of him. Not when they weren't playing their parts.

He leaned closer. "What did you say, sweetheart? I didn't catch it."

Her hands gripped his sleep T-shirt and tugged, big handfuls he had no hope of escaping. Not that he wanted to. The scent of sleepy woman underlay the lingering scent of her soap—some floral scent he discovered was his favourite perfume when Anna wore it.

Locked in an unexpected embrace and balancing at an awkward angle on the edge of her bed, Jack hesitated before scooping her into his arms. He eased around until his back was against the headboard and held her close. Her head dropped onto his shoulder, sleep-heavy and warm. One hand released its hold on his shirt and dropped into her lap while the other clung as though it would never let him go.

Not that he wanted to let her go either, but he faced a dilemma. His promise to Anna that he wouldn't intrude in her space versus the comfort she seemed to derive from his presence.

A muffled sound that could have been 'S'nice' escaped in a puff of air across his chest. It was hard to tell when her face was buried against his neck and her warm breath on his skin made him think things that definitely weren't part of the deal she'd signed up to. Her grip on his shirt slackened, but she snuggled close.

Snuggled, and he liked it!

A longing he hadn't known existed filled him. What would it be like if their relationship was real and he had the right to hold her like this every night?

Following fast on the heels of that came the thought, *What would she think if she woke like this, in his arms?*

He drew in a deep breath, committing the scent of her to

memory, before he lay her down and tried to ease out of her bed. Her grip tightened on his shirt, fierce in intent despite the fact she was asleep.

Her subconscious need and his desire battled with what he knew he had to do.

Absence versus presence. Should he go—or stay?

Either way he was damned.

***

Aware of air wafting at regular intervals across her face, Anna pushed into the welcome warmth at her back and buried her nose beneath the doona. Relaxed and refreshed, she decided in that half-waking, half-sleeping state, she must have slept well. Luxuriating in the warmth, she wriggled closer . . .

Her eyes sprang open.

He couldn't . . . he hadn't, had he?

But the evidence of Jack going back on his word poked her in the back. Heart in her mouth, she tried to ease away and look over her shoulder to confirm what her body already knew. An arm heavy as lead pinned her to him, against him, against . . .

Fearful anger propelled her away. "What the hell do you think you're doing?" With an almighty thrust, she pushed his arm off and rolled onto the other side of the bed.

Jack's eyes cracked open with the look of someone coming out of a deep sleep. "Wha—?"

She yanked the pillow out from behind her and hit his head. "You bast—"

He grabbed her wrist as she raised the pillow for a second blow. "What are you doing?"

"What am I doing? What are you doing—here, in my bed—where you said you'd never come unless I invited you? I didn't invite you."

He took the pillow from her, tossed it off the end of the bed and sat up against the headboard. Without answering her, he rubbed both hands across his face and through sleep-tousled hair before doing the wide-eyed blinking of the newly awoken. "I knew it would be like this."

"Are you blaming me for this? How do you think this is my fault?" Anger built in her chest, burning so hot she threw off the doona and kneeled up, glaring at him.

Instead of quailing under her glare, or melting into a puddle from the heat of her anger, Jack merely sighed. "It's nobody's fault, Anna. You screamed during the night and I came in expecting to find an intruder in your room. I tried to wake you. You grabbed my shirt and wouldn't let go and—I tried to leave."

She snorted at the absurd idea. Last time she believed him because of a dim recollection of falling asleep on the sofa bed. His bed. But now? *Twice is one too many coincidences.* "How hard did you try?"

He let his head fall against the headboard and it dawned on her—slowly and too late—he looked tired. Bags under his eyes and faint shadows suggested he'd slept poorly. He hadn't made a move on her, and—now she looked—either side of the V-neck of his sleep T-shirt, two distinct hand-sized wrinkles backed up his story. She narrowed her gaze on them. The awful feeling she'd wrongly jumped down his throat—again—began to grow.

One hand rose and touched the wrinkled material. "Oh, God, did I do that?"

He tipped his head down and looked where her fingers brushed his shirt.

She snatched her hand away and curled her hands together on her lap.

"Yes, Anna, I reckon that's from where you grabbed me and held tight."

"Why?" She couldn't trust herself around Jack. Clearly her subconscious had been working overtime while she slept, fuelling the attraction she recognised and had been fighting. And losing the battle, it seemed.

"I thought you were having a nightmare. Maybe because of

the date?”

The date? *The date!*

Her gaze flew to the calendar and the red circle around today.

“Yes.” Behind the whispered syllable, memory of the whole terrible nightmare crashed back around her. But stronger than that was the sense of safety that had followed. Was that when Jack had checked on her; held her? *When she'd suddenly felt* not *alone.*

Jack flipped the covers back and got out of her bed. “I'll leave you in peace and go put the kettle on. I have a feeling I'm going to need a lot of coffee today.” His voice came to her as though from a distance, through a fog of mixed reaction and the lingering thread of bad memories.

While she stumbled around her feelings for Jack—around the shock and surprise of their unlooked-for connection—he disappeared down the hallway. Part of her still felt the pull towards wallowing in the anniversary. That damned red circle sat like a malevolent eye cursing her. But another part, newer and stronger, with fleeting hints of optimism, drew her out of bed and into the kitchen.

Jack was leaning on the bench staring through the window as she entered. In the background, a rising hum of water coming to the boil masked her approach until she touched his shoulder. When he turned, the look in his eyes was unexpected.

Almost sad, she thought. “I did it again, didn't I?”

A muscle jumped in his cheek, but he simply looked at her.

“Jack, I'm sorry. I—” She looked away, unable to hold his gaze. Self-realisation was uncomfortable and this morning's was a major wake-up call. Her tongue touched the corner of her mouth and she sucked in a deep breath. “You know that whole *It's-not-you-it's-me* thing? Well, it really is me. You asked the other night if my parents had gone to counselling after the home invasion, but you didn't ask about me. Because I didn't tell you the whole story."

She clenched her hands and he covered them with his and drew her onto a seat at the table. "Anna, you don't have to tell me anything you don't want to. If it makes you uncomfortable—"

She shook her head. "No, I think you need to know. It's why I'm so awful to you."

"You haven't been awful."

"I have. I've jumped down your throat for no good reason, except . . . There is a reason. Something I haven't dealt with."

"Let me make the coffee first." He spooned granules into two mugs, taking his time, which gave her a chance to think about how to tell him. Sharing the darkest part of her life was never going to be easy, but something about Jack made it feel possible.

By the time he set a mug in front of her, she was as ready as she'd ever be. She sipped her coffee and then wrapped both hands around the mug and held it on the table. "I was trying to work out the best way to say this, but I think it's like a sticking plaster; easier if you just rip it off fast. So—you know my father was injured in the home invasion and that my mother is still so frightened she can't stay outside after dark; she locks herself inside before sunset. But I haven't told you what happened when I—" Her breath caught on the jagged edge of words she hadn't spoken to anyone since the police report and court appearance. Words that assumed hideous proportions when she simply thought them.

Would she be able to go on after setting them free?

Would Jack see her differently, treat her differently when he knew?

Jack held out his hand.

She gripped it—and there was another miracle, this voluntary touching after so many months keeping everyone at a distance. Touching Jack, feeling his quiet reassurance flow into her at the contact, she swallowed the lump of anxiety rising like bile in her throat. "I walked in on the thieves just after they'd tied my parents up. One of them grabbed me and . . . assaulted me."

Jack's hand did a quick, involuntary squeeze, tight enough that she winced. "Assaulted you, as in tied you up too?"

She looked down at their joined hands. For most of the past year she'd avoided physical contact with men, and jumped at her own shadow. Fear had held her hostage in her own home for several weeks after the attack, and the city she had once loved became a jungle, a place where even home wasn't safe. And so she'd run, all the way to Lark Creek. Here, fear had held her aloof, apart from a couple of artistic commissions, and tried to rebuild some sort of life.

And then Kaden had shattered her pseudo-peace and brought Jack into her world. And Jack had wrapped her in his warmth and given her a sense of security that she knew would only last until Kaden's uncle was caught and put away. Then, Jack would leave and she would be more alone than before.

But Jack was here now, holding her hand because she'd chosen to let him into her life. She kept holding on, knowing their association had an expiry date. One she feared she would never be ready for.

Finally, she met his gaze. "I was sexually assaulted. That's why I can't—why I don't want—"

"Oh, Anna." He made a move as though to wrap her in his arms, but pulled back before he touched her. "I'm sorry. I can't begin to imagine how hard our charade has been on you."

"In a strange way, I think it's helped. I knew it wasn't real, that we were playing roles. Somehow I was able to deal with that. And I knew by doing it, we were contributing to Kaden's safety. But when we're here in my home, when we aren't acting, my insecurity flares up. That's twice I've unfairly accused you of trying to come on to me. I'm sorry."

He looked at their joined hands, and raised an eyebrow. "If intimacy is an issue for you, how can you bear—this?"

She could feel his hold loosening, letting her go because he thought that was what she wanted, what she needed. But when he no longer held her hand she felt bereft.

Was this wanting when Jack was around a sign she was finally beginning to heal?

That need to hold onto him welled up inside. Not touching Jack now was harder than his touch had been at the start of their roleplay.

"Anna, I'll ask Smithy to come up with a different plan if you like, one that doesn't put you under constant strain having to play a role that you hate."

She thought about it, thought carefully about what life would feel like without Jack in her space. A few days earlier, that would have sounded like heaven, to have her home free from unwanted guests.

But now . . .

"You know, this probably sounds strange after what I just shared, but I'm getting used to it—to you being here. On balance, if you don't mind, I'd like to continue."

Chapter 17

Jack lifted the axe and brought it down on the block of wood. A crack and a thud followed as the piece split in two. One half fell off the chopping block and Jack turned the other piece around and split it again, and then again. As he stacked the newly-cut pieces under the awning beside the wood shed, a sense of satisfaction filled him. Already the evenings were cool and last night they had lit the wood stove in the lounge room, using the last of the previous winter's chopped logs. Jack had pushed the wheelbarrow around the property and Kaden and Anna filled it with deadfall wood and twigs. The Donovans had dumped a trailer load of larger blocks beside the lean-to and Jack offered to chop enough for the evening.

The small pile he'd chopped was enough for the week. He put the axe away, loaded up an armful of chopped wood and carried it inside. "Anna, do you have a bucket for the firewood?"

She emerged from the bathroom, rubbing her wet hair with a lemon-coloured towel. "What was that?" A silky robe in swirling paisley pattern was tied snugly around her waist and her cheeks were pink and damp with heat.

By rights, he shouldn't find that image arousing, but it didn't seem to matter what Anna wore. Jack's fascination with his co-conspirator had been growing since they had butted heads over Kaden that first day at the police station. And since she had opened up about being attacked during the home invasion a year ago, he'd been carefully avoiding touching her. All those casual touches, slinging his arm over her shoulder and dropping light-hearted kisses on her forehead when they were with other people . . . all those actions he hadn't given a second thought to had assumed a different, more damaging slant. And now that he was conscious of not touching her, his fingers itched to stroke her hair, and his arms felt empty without Anna to wrap around.

He looked down at the armload of firewood and over towards the fireplace; anywhere but at Anna in that damned silky robe. "Where do you want the wood? I can stack it on the tiles, but it might be better in a bucket or something." He could imagine the slide of warm silk beneath his fingers, and the scent of Anna fresh from the shower and . . .

The wood shifted in his arms and, as he clutched the sliding load, a long splinter dug into his palm. "Damn it."

"What's the matter?" She came closer.

He set the pile on the tiles and stood, turning his hand towards the dimming light from the windows. "Splinter. It's nothing. Is Kaden back from visiting Graham?"

"He's in his room reading. He came in about half an hour ago, excited about what Graham had shown him. Let me see." She took Jack's hand and tipped it so light fell on it. "I'll get the first aid kit. You—sit there."

"Don't bother. I'm sure I can pull it out without—"

Gently but firmly she pushed him back and into the armchair. "Stop being such a hero. We're going to use tweezers and antiseptic and make sure we get all of the slivers out."

"Yes, ma'am." Without being rude, Jack couldn't think of how else to avoid having Anna touch him.

At least this is her choice. Maybe that makes a difference.

When Anna returned with a small first aid kit, she made him sit next to the desk lamp she'd pulled out for his use the first time he brought a file home from the office. Shining the light on his palm, she held his hand and gently turned it until she was satisfied with the angle before setting to work. She gripped the long splinter and pulled it out, setting the sliver on a piece of lint. Then she tipped his hand back and forth under the light. "There's two more small splinters—see. There and there." She pointed at two small dark spots in his palm.

"They'll work their own way out. I wouldn't worry about them." He made to pull his hand from her grasp.

She tightened her hold on his wrist and tugged his hand back into the light. "Jack Donaldson, if I didn't know better, I'd say you were a scaredy-cat. Don't you want me to go digging around in your palm with my little bitty pair of tweezers?" She clicked the tips of the tweezers together making a soft, tinging sound.

"It isn't that." Despite his office career, his hands weren't soft. Not with the gym workouts he enjoyed. He hadn't felt anything as she removed the largest splinter because his whole being was concentrated on the fragrance of Anna's soap underlying the perfume that was her unique scent. As she bent over his hand, her head close to his face, all he could see, all he could sense, was Anna. Her nearness drove him crazy with need, with wanting her. If she didn't move away, he was afraid—not of her hurting him, but of frightening her with his growing desire to take her in his arms. Knowing how tough physical contact was for her, he refused to inflict more than absolutely necessary. For goodness sake, they weren't in town and there was nobody here to impress with their reunited lovers story.

"Then what is it, Jack?" She looked up into his eyes.

Her pupils were dark and, as he watched, her eyes widened. Was he somehow transmitting his desire?

Shit, shit, shit. Think about something else. Think about the dead snake on the road, or the photo of that cattle truck accident. Don't think about Anna.

He scrunched his eyes shut, but she still held his hand. At last, when the silence stretched beyond hope she'd leave him be, he grated out a reluctant reply. "Geez, Anna. I can't be this close to you without thinking about holding you."

"Then grit your teeth, hold your breath and count to five because I'm getting these last two slippery little suckers out of your palm."

There was one small, quick pinch of his skin, and a longer, drawn out prodding and scraping before she spoke triumphantly. "Got them."

He opened his eyes. She brandished the tweezers aloft like the winner of an Olympic gold medal with their bunch of flowers. Before he could speak, she put the tweezers down and applied a cotton pad to his palm. Three little pricks stung as the antiseptic hit the tiny wounds and then she cleared the used pads into a small bowl.

"All done."

He flicked a glance at his palm and clenched and opened his hand. "Great. Thanks."

"And there's one more thing."

He was halfway out of the armchair, needing to get away from her, when her hand landed on his shoulder and pushed him back down. "What more could there be?"

"Didn't your mother ever reward you for being brave when she dressed your wounds? Mine did, every time."

His mother had kissed his forehead and hugged him, but that wouldn't be on the cards with Anna. "Are you going to give me a red lollipop?"

"There's a thought. I'll be right back." She disappeared into the kitchen.

A moment later, he heard the sound of the pantry door squeaking as she opened it. With Anna gone, the delicious, torturous haze in his brain eased and he added *oil the door* to his mental list of household chores. Along with buying something to store the chopped wood in beside the fireplace. He didn't want to risk another splinter-removal episode.

The sound of Anna's bare feet crossing the wooden floor changed when she stepped onto the rug. She kneeled on the floor in front of him and held out her hand.

It took him a heartbeat or two before he dragged his gaze

from her beautiful hazel eyes to the object in her hand. He laughed. Her treat was cute and unexpected. "A heart-shaped lollipop? Thanks."

"You said it yourself. Brave boys deserve rewards. And before you ask, they were on sale after Valentine's Day."

He ripped the plastic wrapper off the lollipop, but she gripped his wrist as he raised the sweet to his mouth. "You have to close your eyes before you taste it."

She was so close he could see flecks of gold in her eyes. The touch of her hand, the zephyr of her breath across his cheek cut through his resistance. He would do anything she asked, but still the auto-response dropped from his mouth. "Why?"

"Because."

Reluctantly, he closed his eyes, but still she didn't let go of his wrist. With his eyes shut the scent of her floral perfume intensified. A subtle movement of air, and the swish of her silk robe across his arms, a whisper of breath . . .

Anna's lips touched his mouth in a butterfly-soft kiss, beautiful and brief.

He held his breath, unable to believe the kiss had happened, wishing she would repeat the tentative contact. No other kiss had ever touched him like Anna's. As first kisses went, it was neither erotic nor lingering nor an invitation to a night of sex, but it was off the chart.

Because Anna had chosen to kiss *him*.

Her kiss was so much more than a mere touching of lips. Somewhere in their verbal jousting, they had connected in a way that let her feel safe.

Anna's kiss was a statement of trust.

Once upon a time it would have been his chest puffing up in pride. Now, he feared her tentative kiss had touched his heart.

***

Anna sat back on her heels, breathless and exultant at her daring. She'd kissed Jack. Not much of a kiss to be sure, but

127

initiating that intimate contact was liberating. Feeling empowered, she waited, hopeful and yet, uncertain about his response.

He opened his eyes, slowly.

"Jack?"

Stunned was too mild a description for the frozen man in front of her. Watching for some reaction, *any* reaction, a sinking sensation in her stomach sent her groping for the sofa.

His expression gave away little more than the fact she'd taken him by surprise. She'd surprised herself with the impulse, the sudden need to know what his mouth felt like.

"I'm sorry. I shouldn't have done that."

"It's fine. It was unexpected, but—nice." He stood, the lolly treat dangling from his fingers. "I'll take a turn around the perimeter while I eat my lollipop. Goodnight, Anna."

Lying in bed, the doona gripped high beneath her chin, Anna stared through the rectangular windowpanes into the dark night.

Nice! he said?

It was stupid to have kissed him in the first place. How many times had she reminded herself to beware of getting caught up in the reality of their role-play? It was even more stupid to expect a different response, but still . . . *nice!*

Anna glanced at the monitor screens, now on night mode, and sighed.

This whole worrying situation was doing her head in, but one positive about that crazy kiss stood out above all else, even above her mortification over Jack's lack of response. It put the events of last year firmly in the past, where they belonged and shone a light on the future.

I kissed Jack because I wanted to.

It gave her hope she was on the road to recovery.

Chapter 18

Katy Leonard and Travis Roberts sat side by side on her sofa, turning as one and grinning at her. "Anna, Travis and I are engaged!" Katy's face glowed with the love she felt for the man by her side.

"Congratulations! That's wonderful news."

The left side of Travis' face barely moved, a result of his motorbike injury, but his eyes were so expressive Anna almost missed that detail when he met her gaze. "We won't be getting married until next year, but we wanted to ask if you would paint a portrait of us."

"Oh, wow, I'd be honoured." A little daunted too, given Travis' fame on the music scene. His comeback just before Christmas was thanks to Katy refusing to let him hide and the concert had been nationally televised. Media interest in his engagement was sure to be huge. Would that transfer to her little art gallery, if—*no, when*—she got it up and running? "What sort of painting did you have in mind?"

"I'd love you to include Travis' favourite guitar, but other than that, we're really open to your ideas." Katy flicked a glance at Travis and a shy grin suggested she hadn't shared her wish with her fiancé.

Kaden walked into the lounge room, his attention so focused on the tablet in his hand he didn't notice Anna's visitors until he reached the sofa. They turned just as he noticed them and he seemed to shrink against the bow-front, satinwood cabinet. He threw Anna an agitated look, one that combined wariness with apology for walking in on her, a second before Anna signed in reassurance. *Friends. Here to ask for a painting of themselves.*

He tucked the tablet under his arm and signed, *Sorry, didn't know anyone was here,* and edged away before she could introduce him. As he disappeared into his bedroom, Anna was left with the unmistakeable impression he felt threatened by strangers in the house. Had the murder he'd witnessed in his uncle's warehouse made him fearful of even normal people like Katy and Travis, or was it as simple as being caught unaware?

Travis had turned away and his hand rose to his scarred cheek. Katy shook her head and whispered, "It's not you, darling."

Worried that Kaden's behaviour appeared rude, Anna tried to smooth over the awkwardness. "That's—Jed, my brother. Sorry about that. He didn't realise you were here and felt bad for walking in on our conversation. You know what teenage boys can be like."

Travis patted Katy's hand and rolled his eyes. "Don't worry about it. Katy knows all too well what teenagers can be like."

"Tell me about it. I had my nephew here over the Christmas break while my sister and her husband were in Japan. He caused me some heart-stopping moments."

Anna thought hard. She had met Katy's nephew the day she'd delivered the sign for the newly opened B and B. He'd helped the builder dig the hole for the post, but she hadn't talked with him because they'd been focusing on preparing to spread Katy's Gran's ashes. But Anna was sure she'd seen him elsewhere. "Was that the young man who played on stage with you at the Christmas concert?"

"Yes, that was Adam."

"He's got the makings of a good guitarist, and fine taste in music, if I do say so." Travis winked at Katy. "Isn't that right, babe?"

"Whatever you reckon." Katy rolled her eyes and patted his knee. "Travis thinks Adam's taste is great just because he decided he likes country music."

Travis nodded. "Yeah, he's mad keen on playing guitar and bugged me to teach him when I was still barely able to play a basic melody line."

"You've come a long way since then, darling." Katy set a hand on Travis' cheek and gazed into his eyes.

Anna sat separate from the conversation while her visitors shared their silent communion. Seeing them wrapped in one another, oblivious to her in this moment, she began to see how she would paint them. That shared gaze for starters—that had to be included.

"Does your Jed like music, Anna?" Travis was looking at her expecting a response.

Anna blinked, realising she had zoned out in a creative haze. "What was that?"

"What sort of music does Jed like?"

It dawned on Anna that Travis had misinterpreted Kaden's reaction as surprise at seeing his scarred face. He must not have noticed them signing to one another. "He—doesn't listen to music."

Katy shook her head and squeezed her fiancé's hand. "Not now, Trav." She turned back to Anna. "Tell me, do older sisters manage younger brothers better than aunts with nephews?"

Kaden's closed door suggested that wouldn't be the case, even if he were really her brother. "Jed's a good kid. He helps with chores and he watches Jack closely and copies what he does. He tries but—some things are a little more difficult when you're born deaf."

Travis half turned towards where Kaden had stood moments earlier. "Jed's deaf? I'm sorry, Katy. I didn't know or I wouldn't have asked the question."

"It's not a problem, Travis. I just wish there was a way he could enjoy what the rest of us get to experience, but it's not to be. Anyway, back to your painting . . ."

Images of how she might capture the love sparking between her friends began to coalesce in Anna's mind. Travis holding his guitar—clearly the second love of his life after Katy—

and looking down into Katy's eyes as she lay across his lap looking up. "I'll do a few preliminary sketches to discuss ideas with you. Would it be convenient if I brought them around say, next Friday?"

"Babe, isn't that when the caterer is coming?"

"Yes, but that won't take all afternoon. How about around five o'clock? Stay for a barbecue and bring—Jed, is it?"

The idea of taking Kaden out to any social gathering, even a small one, challenged Anna's notion of *safe*. Here at the cottage, surrounded by Graham's all-seeing, all-recording camera net, she had a measure of security. Venturing as far from home as Travis' farm—would that be reasonable in Smithy's book? "That's kind of you, but Jack will be—"

Travis stopped her with a smile. "The more the merrier. Bring him too. Since Katy made me re-enter the world, I've rediscovered how much I enjoy spending time with friends."

"And he cooks a great barbie." Katy turned to Travis. "How about you do your famous marinated pork fillet?"

Travis spread his hands. "Do you like pork, Anna?"

"Love it, and Jack is certainly developing a taste for it. And Jed—" She shrugged, unsure what Kaden thought of pork. "You know what teenage boys' appetites are like."

Katy stood and pulled Travis up beside her. "Great. We'll see you around five on Friday. And thank you for agreeing to do the painting. When Travis suggested the idea, I didn't want anyone but you to do it for us."

"I'm honoured, and thrilled at your trust in me." On impulse, Anna gave Katy a quick hug.

Travis hesitated and then gave her a hug as well before leading the way to the front door. He stopped on the top step and looked up at the corner of the house. "We should get some camera monitoring for our place like Anna's got here. Who installed yours, Anna?"

"Graham Peyton." The camera was small enough she'd

thought it would be unnoticed by most people. Hoping like crazy they didn't ask why she felt the need for such monitoring, she flicked a glance at her watch and took a gamble. "Jack should be home soon if you'd like to stay for a drink?"

"Thanks, but *a certain someone* has a conference call with his manager that I think he's forgotten about." Katy nudged Travis before heading down the stairs.

Travis slung an arm over Katy's shoulders and tossed Anna a casual wave. "Another time maybe. See you later."

A cool late afternoon breeze eddied around Anna before she closed the door. She went to her bedroom and put on a jumper. On the monitor, she could see Travis' ute bouncing over the ruts in her driveway. At the end, Katy jumped out and opened the gate for Travis to drive through just as Jack's car slowed and pulled over on the verge of the road. Travis passed through the gate and pulled alongside Jack's car. Katy left the gate open for Jack and got into the ute, but the vehicles remained stationary as the drivers chatted. With nothing happening, Anna headed back into the lounge and collected the coffee mugs and cake plates and stacked them on a tray.

A few minutes later, Jack drove in and parked. Had Travis told him why they were visiting? Wanting to see Jack's reaction when she shared her news, she hoped not.

She set the tray down on the kitchen bench and held the door open while Jack toed off his shoes and set them on the rack beside the door.

"I just saw Travis and Katy leaving. Pity they couldn't stay for a drink, but they said we're invited over on Friday for a barbie."

"That's right. The three of us are invited over."

"Great, although I'm surprised they didn't text the invitation."

Had he missed her slight emphasis on *the three of us*? Should she raise her concerns about taking Kaden on the visit before she shared her news? Her good mood won. "So—Travis didn't tell you why they were here?"

Jack shrugged. "Just about the barbecue. Was there another reason they called in?"

"There was." Anna took a bottle of red wine from the wine rack and passed it to Jack to open while she plucked two glasses from the cupboard. She took a plate of plastic-wrapped cheese and two dips out of the fridge and peeled the cling wrap from a bowl of biscuits. Having planned to serve some pre-dinner nibbles, she decided to make it festive and got out her one good serving platter.

Jack let out a slow whistle. "This has the feeling of a celebration." He raised an eyebrow as he poured the wine and set the bottle on the table.

Anna raised her glass. "There are things, important things to celebrate. First, Travis and Katy are engaged, and second, they've asked me to paint their engagement portrait."

"Anna, that's wonderful news. Here's to Lark Creek's finest artist. Well done!" He touched his glass to hers. The chink sounded festive. Jack's smile and the look in his eyes sealed it for Anna. Today was her best day in a long time.

She sipped her wine and picked up the platter and carried it into the lounge room. "I'm so excited. I've a few ideas already about how I want to paint them."

Travis followed with the bottle of wine. "Have they given you *carte blanche* over what you do?"

"Pretty much. Katy wants Travis' favourite guitar included, but other than that, they're open to suggestions. I'm taking some sketches over on Friday to discuss with them before the barbecue. One thing though, Jack; I'm starting to feel a bit concerned about Kaden. He looked, maybe not scared exactly, but wary when he walked in on us this afternoon."

Jack scooped dip onto a cracker and popped it into his mouth. He crunched through it, but his attention seemed to turn on the problems of being responsible for a teenager. "Have you had a chance to talk to him about how he's feeling?"

Anna caught her bottom lip on her teeth. "No, and I should have, shouldn't I? But I don't want to say the wrong thing. I'm not a psychologist."

"Sometimes just showing you're willing to listen can be enough."

"You'd think I would have sat down with him to talk at least once in the past couple of weeks. I feel terrible that I haven't."

"We've all had things on our minds and you've had a difficult first anniversary to get through. I'm not surprised talking about Kaden's feelings hasn't been top of your list of priorities. But you've thought of it now. Would it help if I sit with you while you talk to him? I mean, we are in this together. We should share both the care and the wear." He picked up a cube of cheese and added it to a biscuit. "Maybe I can connect with him man to man."

"I'd appreciate that, thanks. I guess I feel a bit out of my depth, not having a brother for real."

"Tell you what, how about I give Rick a call first and see if there's any chance of Kaden doing some carpentry with him at the winery? Give Kaden something to look forward to?"

***

"Great, thanks, Rick." Jack thumbed off his phone and set it on the table. Anna leaned back in her chair, her eyes closing as a sigh escaped that could only be relief. He felt it too, that lifting of spirits when their cobbled-together plan worked. "Thank goodness. Now to tell Kaden what's in store for him."

"And then we'll have that chat. Do you want to leave it until we've eaten?"

"Might be a good idea." Anna opened her eyes and looked directly into Kaden's angry face. He had appeared behind Jack while her eyes were closed, and Jack didn't seem to be aware of his presence.

What is planned for me? Do I get a say?

Aware he'd read her lips, Anna sat up. Wine sloshed onto the table and into the bowl of crackers as she hurried to sign back.

Good things. A friend would like you to help him build some shelves. Would you like to do that?

What friend? The man with scars?

Not him.

Graham? I like him. He showed me where he lives and lots of different woods.

Kaden had returned from a visit with Graham looking happier than she'd ever seen the teenager. He'd sat out by the fire pit until dark, working on a piece of wood with a whittling knife Graham had given to him. In the solitary, secluded life Kaden was forced to live with Anna, Graham had offered him an escape.

He's a good man. But this other friend works at the winery down the road. He's a good man too.

Do you trust him? Isn't he the man who Jack said was in jail?

Anna thought how badly she'd judged Rick when he was newly arrived back in town. Along with most people, she hadn't looked beyond his jail time to see how decent he was. But he'd proved himself when he'd helped Gei and her parents while her father's heart problems stopped him working. It seemed she wasn't alone in making snap judgements based solely on the word *jail*.

He was, but he didn't do what they said he did. Does that worry you?

Kaden tossed the tablet onto the table and dragged a chair out. He sat with a thump that rocked the chair onto its back legs before it crashed to the floor. *What if he's not good, just pretending? What if he knows my uncle?*

Anna frowned. At the deepest level, she knew Rick was good, but the odd link Kaden had drawn between Rick being in jail and Ferdy Hickman was disturbing.

Graham is his father. You like and trust him, don't you? She continued to sign and speak for the benefit of both males.

"Jack, Kaden is concerned that Rick might know his uncle. Why would he say that? There's definitely something about this situation that's got him worried."

Jack sat forward and looked at Kaden as he asked, "Why do you think that?"

Kaden gave Jack a pitying look, as though the question was ridiculous. *He's got people in his pocket; people in important jobs. Money changed hands.*

How do you know this? Turning to Jack, Anna added, "It's not the sort of comment I would expect from a boy his age."

I lip-read sometimes when they came to visit. They knew I was deaf and didn't take care what they said in front of me. They thought I was a moron because I couldn't hear or speak. Anna translated for Jack, but her attention was on Kaden's face—on the anger burning in his eyes.

"I'm worried, Jack. It sounds serious."

"And strangely probable." He rubbed his thumb across his lower lip as he picked up his phone. "I think we should let Smithy know about Kaden's comments. It seems there's more to this case than murder."

While Jack phoned Smithy Anna and Kaden served a lamb casserole from the slow cooker, but as they sat around the table, Anna's appetite fled. Her stomach roiled as it always did when her anxiety levels peaked. She dropped her fork onto her barely-touched food, set her elbows either side of the plate and rested her chin on her hands. "Does Smithy think there might be anything to his claims?"

Jack set his fork down and leaned back, pushing his plate away.

Almost nothing affected Jack's appetite, but the fact he hadn't eaten much was enough to drag the clawing fear up Anna's throat. The little she had eaten threatened to return and she grabbed her glass of water, sipping and praying for it to calm the revolution going on in her stomach.

"He thinks if Kaden can identify any of the important people who visited his uncle's home, it could open a whole new line of inquiry. He's going to visit again with photos of people who might fit Kaden's description of *important people*.

"The fact is this latest development worries me more than when it was just keeping Kaden off the radar. If he can identify a big name, high profile player—"

Anna exhaled a long drawn-out breath. "We're all in real danger."

"Anna, no matter what, we have to stay off the radar. I know Kaden understands he can't contact any of his friends, but we should add no more browsing the internet as well. And if this painting for Travis includes media attention, we have to keep Kaden right out of it. At any cost."

Chapter 19

As Jack passed the sign to Thornyhill Farm and turned onto the driveway, he felt himself relaxing a little. After Kaden's revelation about his uncle bribing senior people in key positions, Smithy had suggested Anna and Kaden—minus Jack—should begin a series of moves, never stopping longer than a few days in any one place.

Although nervous, Anna had protested. "Jack and I have put a lot into building up our cover here in Lark Creek. We've created the story of our renewed romance alongside the visit of my little brother. People are happy for us. And a lot of people now recognise Kaden as my little brother, Jed; they've seen us signing in conversation together and nobody has a reason to think he's anyone but who we said he is."

Jack had backed her up. "We've got surveillance all over the property and Graham keeping an eye out from the ridge. At the moment, I think we feel safer staying with the known."

Smithy had grumbled, but Jack suspected that was more for Anna's benefit. When he walked his friend to his car, he probed for the truth. "Is it fair to say you secretly agree with Anna's assessment of our situation?"

Smithy's eyes narrowed. "Either you know me too well or your understanding of my work has improved out of sight. Yes, your girl is right. Keep your heads down and Hickman isn't likely to find his nephew."

Your girl. He liked the sound of that. In spite of the dangers, one traitorous part of Jack was glad Smithy agreed with their decision. After only three weeks, still the idea of Anna leaving without him would have punched a huge hole in his life.

"Right, we'll keep a low profile and go on as before."

"I doubt that."

"What do you mean?"

Smithy snorted and clapped a hand on Jack's shoulder. "Have you looked in a mirror lately? You'll never be the same as before; you're falling for her. It's in your voice, the way you talk about her, the look in your eyes when you mention her name and when you look at her . . . old son, I'd say you're a goner and the sooner you realise you're no longer *playing* the role of her lover, the easier you'll find life with her. Keep it honest."

Aware of Anna's eye for detail, after that conversation Jack had watched every word he'd spoken to her. He thought about staying late in the office as a means of self-preservation, but that defeated the purpose of him living in Anna's home. And so he had taken himself off for evening patrols around the property to gain breathing space.

But tonight, getting out of the house felt like a breath of fresh air.

He parked his car beside Anna's ancient station wagon, wrenched off his tie and tossed it onto the passenger seat, and got out of the car. The aroma of meat and onions cooking on a barbecue drifted on the evening breeze. For the first time in days, Jack's appetite returned and his stomach rumbled.

He followed his nose to an outdoor area still under construction. The skeleton of a pergola was in place with a pile of lengths of wood stacked neatly behind the structure. Next to it was a brick barbecue with a metal plate long enough to hold food for half the town in one go. Both pergola and barbecue sat on a brick floor spiralling out from a central pattern like a giant snail shell.

Travis stood at the barbecue wielding a pair of tongs and an egg flip, while Katy and Anna sat side by side on a rustic log bench. Kaden was throwing a stick for an excited Border Collie puppy and tussling with it for possession on the odd occasion the pup brought the stick back. The scene was idyllic, and the knot in

Jack's stomach eased.

"Hi, sorry I'm late."

Travis looked up and tossed him a can of beer. "Not so late there aren't a few cans left."

Jack caught the can and wisely refrained from opening it immediately. "Smells good. Pork?"

"Yeah. Katy loves it and apparently it's one of Anna's favourites. Me, I like a thick steak. There's plenty of both."

Anna and Katy stopped their conversation to greet him and Katy gestured towards the can in his hand. "I see Travis has taken care of the essentials. Pull up a pew."

Jack looked around for another log or a chair, but Anna moved along the bench and patted a space beside her.

"Join me if you like."

"I like." He leaned down and kissed her cheek—*there was an audience of two, after all*—and sat. The puppy raced up to him, dropped the stick at his feet and began sniffing his shoes. He scratched its head and under its chin. "What's your name, fella?"

Katy grinned. "Other than *Did-you-eat-my-sandals*, her name is Cassie."

Travis added, "Cass is Katy's dog, for company when I have to be away from home. And she steals shoes so watch your feet."

The pup found Jack's shoelace, gripped it in sharp little teeth and began tugging, accompanied by a low growling.

"I see what you mean. Guess she likes the taste of leather." He scooped her onto his lap where she curled up and fell asleep. Kaden slumped on another log bench and began peeling strips of bark off another stick. It occurred to Jack the boy was lonely and he promised himself he'd find ways to spend more time with him. Maybe they could climb the lower part of the ridge on the weekend and visit Graham again.

Anna touched his shoulder and he forgot about the pup and Kaden as he fell into her smile. "Busy day at the office, darling?"

"A bit." Anna in role was totally convincing. As Jack looked into her warm hazel eyes the lines between pretence and reality blurred. It would be easy to overstep the mark and imagine their relationship slipping into real life. Easy and comfortable. No wonder he was falling for her.

Falling? Smithy's parting words crashed over Jack. It wasn't real. *They* as a couple did not exist. If he didn't remember that, if he let fantasy consume him, he would make life difficult for Anna. For both of them.

Once the image had settled in his imagination, no amount of rubbing his thumb and finger over tired eyes could wipe it away.

He leaned away from Anna and ripped the tab off the beer can. Smithy was right, damn him. It was too late. Jack had already fallen for Anna and there was no going back.

*****

As Jack edged away from her, Anna feared some new development had occurred. All week he'd been tense—since Smithy's visit, now she thought about it. The two men had stood beside Smithy's hire car and talked for a while before the agent left. When Jack returned to the house, his hooded gaze had settled on her and she'd felt the change between them, a widening chasm she had no idea how to bridge.

He no longer touched her when they were alone, not since she'd shared what had happened to her. She should be grateful Jack was thoughtful and careful; considerate and respecting her need for distance once he knew what she'd endured last year.

Instead, she missed the little touches, their fingers brushing as they worked together in the kitchen. Missed the connection between them. She'd tried to let him know she was okay with what most people considered normal interaction between couples.

For goodness sake, she'd kissed him!

How could he misread that? Tonight it seemed he'd momentarily forgotten the distance he'd maintained all week when he kissed her cheek. That flash of pleasure in his eyes as their gazes connected had given her hope and she'd touched him. Set a hand on his shoulder, slid it over his shirt and felt the muscles in his back ripple in response.

And then a shutter had come down and he moved away from her. Not so far their friends would remark on it, but the distance between them was a gulf.

"Jack?" Her voice dropped to little more than a whisper. "You can put your arm around me if you like."

"No need. Here comes Katy with more food. I'll go and chat to Travis." He stood and stepped towards the barbecue.

"Jack—" Unable to stop herself, she reached for his hand.

"Don't, please Anna. Don't push it." There went that muscle in his jaw again, jumping like it had a life of its own.

"You're so tense. What's happened? Has Kaden's uncle done—"

He frowned as though that was the last thing he expected to hear, and shook his head. "No, nothing like that. Everything's quiet from that quarter."

"Then what is it, tell me?"

He looked down at their joined hands as though surprised to see them together, and sighed. "Can we not do this now?"

"When then?"

"When we get home. We can talk then." He joined Travis at the barbecue and began chatting about the puppy and the pergola construction.

Anna raised her glass and drank a mouthful of wine before jumping to her feet and joining Katy. Something was wrong, but she wasn't going to get any more from Jack. Fixing a smile on her face, she set her wine glass on the checked tablecloth and turned to her host. "Tell me what else you want brought out from the house and I'll help. We've got to earn our supper."

***

Jack packed his work files into his briefcase and switched on the table lamps in the lounge. If he was going to talk with Anna, he didn't want to do it in the glare of the overhead light. He dropped the briefcase on top of his bedding in the corner and glared at the pile. That there was his life, a limbo of bedding and work files and not much else.

Why hadn't he just agreed he'd had a hard day and was tired instead of promising to talk?

Because he hated seeing Anna worry, hated the hurt look in her eyes when he pulled away.

Damn it, Jack sucked at the whole relationship thing, the talking about feelings stuff. He pushed aside the curtain and peered down the slope. The familiar shape of Hughie munching his way along Anna's fence line was caught in the headlights as Rory's farm ute drove up the road from town.

Jack was an idiot for offering a talk with Anna. Talking through problems—that was a whole different game. He could talk his way through problems until—until Hughie ate his way home to the dairy farm. But feelings scared the bejesus out of him.

There, he'd acknowledged his weakness. Why did he have to tell Anna anything? The possibility that telling her of his feelings would disturb her peace of mind was real. He could just mention 'pressure of work' and leave it at that. She didn't need to know that sharing the same space and guarding against his every inclination to touch her was winding him tighter than a coiled spring.

Anna walked into the lounge room and held up a bottle of brandy and two glasses. "Do we need liquid courage for this?"

"There's no courage at the bottom of a bottle, but a nightcap would be nice." At least holding a glass would give him something to do with his hands.

She poured the drinks and handed a glass to him. He took it, careful not to touch her hand, and sat in an armchair.

Anna tucked her legs up beside her on the sofa—*his bed. Don't go there.*

"So—is there any news about the investigation?"

"Not that I know of. Smithy said he'd keep us informed. I haven't heard from him since his last visit." Jack sipped his brandy, welcoming the burn in his throat.

"Good, that's one less thing to worry about." She lowered her gaze to her glass and slowly swirled the liquid inside but didn't drink.

In the low light of the lamps, he could hide from Anna, but her downcast gaze also meant he couldn't get a read on her expression or how she was feeling. "There's nothing to worry about."

"And yet you're tense, more stressed than I've ever seen you, and it's only been since I told you about the assault. You see me differently and it's changed how you treat me." She wasn't accusing him, but a hint of hurt underlay her comment. It was so far from what he'd expected, from his self-indulgent, egotistical focus, and he was ashamed of himself.

"Of course it has. God, Anna, I'm not a monster. I don't want to do anything that makes you uncomfortable."

"And yet, you are."

He stared at her. Incomprehension sat like a fog in his brain, wrapping around his ability to reason. "I've tried not to touch you, Anna. I know you don't like it. I'm sorry if I've slipped up or done anything to—"

"Jack, I kissed you. *I—kissed—you.* Do you know how it makes me feel to have you do nothing to reciprocate?"

He sat there, blinking like a—*like a blinking idiot.* "Reciprocity implies a desire to do the same for the other party." *Great comeback, duh. Spout legalese at her.*

Her tongue touched the corner of her mouth. "Right, okay, now I get it—the same desire doesn't exist. I'm sorry. I guess I misread your—" She sucked in a shuddery breath. "Your interest in me. Excuse me please. I'm going to bed."

Anna surged to her feet like a jack-in-the-box, or a slinky reaching for the next step. Her glass landed on the side table with a bang he feared might crack the base. As she swept around the end of the sofa, his frozen brain thawed enough to take hold of her wrist. She stopped with a jerk and even in the low light he saw a shimmer of moisture in her eyes.

He was definitely an idiot. No matter how he tried, he managed to do or say the wrong thing to Anna. "You misunderstood me."

"I thought you were pretty clear but explain it to me without the jargon. In one syllable, yes or no—do you want to kiss me?"

"Yes, but Anna, the problem is I don't just want to kiss you. I could fill an hour just kissing you—all over—but I don't want to *just kiss you*. Is that clear enough?"

She sank onto the footstool beside his armchair and looked into his eyes. Captured by his hold on her hand, her fingers trembled within his. "You want to have sex with me?"

"Not quite."

She frowned and he hastened to make sure she knew precisely what his intentions were.

"I want to make love to you. There's a big difference."

She sucked in a breath, but when their gazes connected, he saw no fear in her eyes. "That's a lot of touching, skin on skin." Taking hold of his hand she dropped a kiss onto his palm before placing his hand against her cheek and closing her eyes.

Jack hardly dared breathe. That Anna would choose to touch him rather than recoil from his touch was a marvel. Another was her cheek, soft and warm beneath his palm, but a single tear escaped from the corner of her eye, landing on his thumb. "Anna?"

"Ssh, I'm seeing if my body and mind are in agreement about you." Slowly, she rubbed her cheek against his hand.

"And?"

Her eyes opened and when she smiled at him it was like sunshine after a week of rain. She glanced at the sofa and touched his cheek. "I think—your place or mine?"

Chapter 20

Anna woke knowing exactly where she was and that Jack was in her bed. Waking with her nose buried in his neck was the nicest way to greet the day. She didn't want to move. Instead, she inhaled his warmth and the scent of him and thinking if she could stay like this for the entire day, she would.

"Good morning, sleepyhead." Jack turned his head and dropped a kiss on her forehead. "I can hear movement outside. I reckon even Kaden is up before us."

Feeling warm and safe, she sat up and reached for her phone. Thumbing it on she stared in disbelief at the screen. "It's nine o'clock! You'll be late for work." She lunged out of bed and grabbed her robe. A hint of self-consciousness flickered through her as she turned her back, shoved her arms into the sleeves and tied the sash belt. Silly, after spending the night in Jack's arms, but there it was. *It would take time to get used to waking beside Jack. But how many mornings would they have before Kaden was safe and their roleplay at an end?*

Pushing aside her negative thoughts, she put on a bright smile and turned back to Jack. "I'll put the coffeepot on while you shower if you like."

"I'm all for coffee in bed—and a repetition of last night's activities if you're *interested*. But Anna, it's Saturday. We have the weekend ahead of us." She looked at him then, really looked.

Jack had tousled hair and no shirt, a wicked grin and a glint in his eyes that did her heart good. He pulled himself up, put his hands behind his head and leaned against the bedhead. "If you like what you see, you're welcome to come back and join me, coffee or no coffee."

"I'm tempted, in spite of your inflated ego. Last night was—"

"The best night of my life, Anna."

Soft as his words were, they echoed in her mind and heart. There and then she realised she was falling for Jack, the lawyer who had changed her mind about him by what he did, not what he said.

Although that last comment of his was going to take a helluva lot to beat.

"Wow, you really know how to make an impression on a woman."

"There's only one woman I want to impress. I hope after last night you know that's you." He held out one hand.

She took it and allowed him to draw her down beside him. "I'm starting to. Just give me time to get used to everything."

"Take all the time you want, but give me hope when all this is over, we won't be—over, that is. I don't want you going anywhere without me."

"Sounds like a promise of more of last night right there. Hold that thought while I brew some coffee."

He pulled her in for a quick kiss that she found impossible to end. By the time Jack released her, the sound of banging pots and pans from the kitchen filtered into her consciousness. "I think Kaden might need help out there. Back soon."

She pulled her robe on again, tightened the sash and headed for the kitchen. Kaden was holding up two pans, one in each hand, and looking from one to the other. He set both on the table and asked, *Which one for pancakes? I remember you said each pan had a different use.*

Her gaze fell on a shaker bottle of pancake mix sitting on the bench before she pointed to the pan beside his left hand. *That one. Like some help?*

Kaden shook his head. *Directions are on the label. Want*

some when they're cooked?

Yes please. I'll make coffee.

Pleased with Kaden's initiative, she was happy that, when he left her care, he would do so with some basic cooking skills. He hadn't been taught any life skills by his uncle and the one sure thing was that he had no other family of his own to look after him. Who knew where he would end up once his uncle was in prison?

She filled the kettle and plugged in the coffee grinder beside her electric percolator. *Do you remember your parents?*

Hazy, like fuzzy photos. I was three when their car skidded over the edge of the mountain. My uncle turned up and claimed me from the police. He peered at the bubbles popping on the top of the first pancake and looked at her. *Is it ready to flip?*

Yes.

He turned the pancake over and set a timer on his phone as Jack walked into the kitchen.

Jack had pulled on a T-shirt and boxers, but it was clear he'd just got out of bed. He patted Kaden on the back and leaned over the pan, sniffing appreciatively. "Good man. Perfect breakfast."

Kaden slid the cooked pancake onto a plate. Before he poured the next dollop of batter into the pan, he looked from Jack to Anna and grinned. *It's about time you two got real.*

What?

Jack wasn't in his bed last night. Finally. Kaden gave her a thumbs-up, picked up the container and poured another serving of batter into the pan.

Anna stared at the teenager, aware of heat creeping up her cheeks. Jack stepped in beside her as she turned away, trying to hide her flaming face.

"Let me guess, Kaden just put you and me together and got the right answer?"

"Yes. How did you know?"

He ran a finger down her cheek. "It's fine, Anna. He knows

our cover story. He'll just be thinking it's now real. Does it worry you he knows?"

She picked up the packet of coffee beans, but stopped before she opened it and looked at him. "Not really. I don't know why I'm blushing."

"Maybe because it's new and you've just got out of the bed where we made love half the night."

Glancing up at him from under her lashes, Anna could feel a grin tugging at her mouth. "And now you've put that image in my head I won't stop thinking about it all through breakfast."

"Good. Hmm, isn't it lucky Rick wants Kaden's help this morning?"

##

Anna and Jack waved to Kaden before they left him with Rick and some serious lengths of wood. Kaden had run his hands along the grain and grinned when Rick handed over a spare tool belt. Anna turned and walked backwards along the smooth driveway. She could see Rick showing Kaden how to measure and cut a piece of wood. The smile hadn't left Kaden's face.

"You're not having second thoughts about dropping Kaden off, are you?"

"I think your suggestion was excellent on several levels." She rested her hand on Jack's arm and kept walking backwards, confident he wouldn't let her fall.

Jack grinned. "Kaden looked happier than I've ever seen him. I was thinking of asking if it's convenient to take him to visit Graham again, maybe tomorrow. He might help Kaden find some wood to make those shelves you were talking about. What do you think?"

She stopped, slid one hand around Jack's neck and pulled his head down, kissing him for an answer.

"I'll take that as a yes, shall I?"

"You'd better." She turned around and linked her arm through Jack's. As new as their relationship was, it felt right, like coming home should feel. "Jack, can I paint you?"

A flare of interest lit his eyes. "Paint me, as in paint *me*? What are you going to use—whipped cream?"

Anna snorted. "Dream on, my lad. Cream doesn't feel nice on the skin, and besides, eating that amount of cream would make me sick. Although strawberry ice cream might be worth trying. Hmm."

"Want me to go to the supermarket?"

"I didn't suspect you of having a one-track mind, Jack Donaldson. No, I don't want you to go to the supermarket, not yet. I want to sketch you first and then paint *your picture*."

"Ah, right. Okay. But only if you agree to do my choice of activity this afternoon. Deal?"

Giving up control in uncharted territory caused a flare of anxiety before Anna reminded herself; she had chosen to trust Jack because he'd shown himself to be worthy of her trust. Curiosity won. "What did you have in mind?"

"Guess you'll just have to wait and see. But I promise you'll enjoy yourself."

Wicked possibilities flitted through Anna's mind, distracting her all the way home. Jack stood by the fire pit waiting patiently while she set up her easel and picked up a piece of charcoal. Finally she looked at him. "I'm ready. Okay, sit on the log and look towards the ridge."

He sat, elbows resting on his knees and tipped his head up. "Like this?"

Studying the angles, Anna shook her head. "Can you rest one elbow on that raised end and stretch your legs out. Maybe cross your ankles. I want you looking relaxed, not disappointed."

"I'll tell you what would relax me—"

"Later. Behave yourself now and we'll both get a reward." She began with broad strokes, setting the lines and angles of Jack's body on paper. He was a good-looking man with a body he kept fit and in shape . . . her imagination took flight. A series of drawings of Jack in various stages of undress, unconscious of any audience . . .

"How's it going there?"

Anna blinked and focused back on her sketch. While her mind had been off in fantasy land, her fingers had captured the essence of Jack in charcoal. "Almost done." She added a little more shading beneath his chin and a few more lines to the jeans wrapped lovingly around his long legs, and set the charcoal down. "You can relax now."

***

Jack doubted he'd ever relax completely while even a slim possibility existed of Kaden's uncle coming for them. No matter how certain Smithy was, or how many times Jack considered their preparations, nothing felt one hundred-percent watertight. But letting his niggling sense of doom overshadow their relationship wasn't about to happen. Anna had had more than her share of trouble and sorrow. He refused to let his concerns affect her further.

He slipped his arms around Anna's waist and peered over her shoulder at her sketch of him. Even in the rough lines her talent and eye for detail were evident. "Yep, that looks like me. So—I was on my best behaviour and I seem to recall being on a promise."

She leaned against him and wrapped her arms over his. "So you were."

"Shall I go into town and buy ice cream?" Rick had offered to give Kaden lunch so they could continue working through the afternoon and finish the job. By Jack's reckoning that left two, maybe three hours for him and Anna to—

From his pocket the vibration of his phone intruded. Anna felt it too and pulled away so he could take the phone out.

"Who is it?"

He looked at the screen and his gut clenched. "Smithy." Who never rang without reason and stuck to prearranged times with a fervour approaching the religious. "I'd better see what he wants. I wouldn't mind a coffee if you could put the kettle on please?"

"Sure." Anna frowned but headed off to the kitchen before Jack answered the call. "Tell me what's happened."

"Geez, mate, I thought he must already have got there and found you when you didn't answer. Have you looked at social media this morning?"

"We had better things to do. Who, what and where?" He turned the speaker on as he walked slowly towards the cottage. The *who* had to be Hickman. Nobody else would be interested in them.

"It started on Twitter. That singer bloke and his fiancée posed for a selfie with their caterer who posted to their account and tagged the clients. Kaden and Anna are visible in the background. Engaged, Travis Roberts is famous enough for the post to have garnered plenty of hits and now the post is trending."

"Shit. Where to now?" Jack's stroll turned into a sprint and he jumped up the steps onto the back veranda.

"We don't know for sure but there was movement, a gathering of some sort late last night at the home of Hickman's lieutenant. We're assuming worst case scenario."

Jack pushed the kitchen door open and Anna spun around as the door hit the wall. Their gazes met as Smithy's voice came through the speaker.

"Hickman may be on his way out there. Get them out now."

Chapter 21

The teaspoon clattered into the sink from Anna's nerveless fingers. She gripped the cold metal edge as her vision shrank to a narrow band of light. Then Jack was behind her, holding her and murmuring something in her ear. Words without meaning, sounds making no sense.

Jack eased her onto a chair, filled a glass with water and thrust it into her hand. Water slopped onto the table before she steadied the glass with her other hand and sipped. Carefully she lowered the glass. "How did he find us?"

"Social media—Twitter. Smithy doesn't know for sure, but he strongly recommends we leave straightaway."

"I'll get our backpacks. They've been packed since this all started, but I'd hoped never to have to use them." Anna rose, feeling like a robot responding to someone else's commands. Maybe that was good because right now her brain didn't feel like it could add one plus one.

Jack followed her into the bedroom. Suddenly he grabbed her arm and pointed at the monitors. "Too late, they're here."

A dark grey SUV had stopped at the gate and a hefty-looking male got out of the passenger seat to open it. Jack heard her soft gasp, and saw the colour drain from her cheeks.

"Come on. We've got to go, now. Out the back through Rory's place." Jack shouldered his backpack and Kaden's, gripped Anna's hand and raced out the back door.

They ran past the cover of the olive and wattle grove, past the garden shed, under the shade of the Donovans' century-old Moreton Bay fig and up the fence line towards the ridge.

"What about Kaden?" Anna's breath sawed in her throat

and her words jerked from her mouth as she ran hard and fast.

"Not now." Jack didn't slow until they reached the lower slopes of the ridge. He stopped behind some bushes and tucked her in behind him. Breathing heavily, he pulled out his phone and scrolled quickly through his contacts. "First, I'll let Smithy know, then I'll call Rick. I think he suspects just enough of our situation to hide Kaden for now. Maybe he can sneak him up to join us under cover of dark."

Anna sank to the ground, her back pressed against a sapling, and peered through the bushes. *Had they been spotted? How much did Hickman know? Had Graham seen the arrival of—*

Jack ended his call to Smithy and Anna tugged his arm. "Graham might have seen what's happening. Shall I call him?"

"Good idea. Ask him about getting Kaden out of the winery while I get in touch with Rick. Maybe we can co-ordinate something now."

Anna's fingers fumbled with sweat and fear, but she found Graham's number and pressed it.

He answered without preamble, his voice low and reassuring. "I'm watching the men from the SUV. They've reached the cottage and they're encircling it. Amateurs, the lot of them. I lost sight of you and Jack when you turned left at the top of the Donovan farm. Where are you now?"

"At the start of the path on the lower slope. Graham, Kaden is over at the winery with Rick." His absence felt like failure on her part, but what else could they have done?

"I know, lass. That's the best place for him for now. Rick will keep him safe and out of sight."

"But we're going to have to get him out of Lark Creek. Jack talked to Smithy but I don't know what they decided."

Jack looked at her and pointed at her phone. "Tell Graham I'll add him to the conversation with Rick."

She passed on the message and rang off.

Jack joined Graham to the conversation with his son, and

Graham took charge. "Okay, gents, this is the plan."

***

"Jack, can you join us for a war council?" Jack looked up from packing a few basic supplies from Graham's store of food into another backpack. They would travel light and fast through the night, but Graham and Rick still hadn't settled on the best escape route.

"Coming." He left Kaden with the last few items to pack and joined the father and son who were saving their bacon. "What have you got?"

Graham pointed out the only vehicular route from the cottage. "Your cars are still parked at the cottage. Hickman's goons have hidden one of theirs around the back, probably with the idea in mind that you're visiting friends nearby. They'll plan to surprise you when you return."

Anna peered over Jack's shoulder. Her fingers trembled slightly as she leaned on him. "Thank goodness you installed those cameras, Graham, and that suggestion to keep the gate closed stalled them long enough for us to get away. I won't sleep for imagining what they would have done if they'd caught us."

Jack's throat constricted. Five minutes more and he and Anna would have been in her bedroom, oblivious to the monitors. Allowing his desire for her to overshadow attention to their environment had nearly cost them dearly. He wouldn't let that happen again.

Rick pointed to the winery entrance a little way down the road from Anna's driveway. "One possibility is for us to lead you down to the winery under cover of dark and I'll drive you out. However, I did a reconnaissance drive through town before I brought Kaden up here. There are unfamiliar cars parked at these two points. Chances are they'll manufacture an excuse—a flat tyre or an open bonnet suggesting engine trouble—and expect any vehicle coming from Ridge Lane to stop and help them."

Graham slipped seamlessly into his son's narrative.

"They'll expect you to try to get out by car but they've effectively boxed you in. Any car that doesn't stop for them will be followed or checked somewhere further down the road."

Jack bent over the map, squinting without his glasses, which were on Anna's bedside table. The more remote location of Anna's cottage had given them a false sense of security and they'd relied too much on Hickman having no idea which direction his nephew had taken. He had trusted his friend. Surely Smithy wouldn't have let them stay there if there was only one way out.

"So while it looks like we're trapped like rats on a sinking ship, I reckon there must be another way out. "He leaned closer and pointed. "What about down to the creek and along the bank towards Travis' farm? Surely the road to his place wouldn't be watched?"

Graham and Rick pored over the topographical map, tracing alternative routes off the ridge to the creek. Father and son glanced at one another and Rick shook his head. "Maybe you could make it along the bank, but moving quietly through this patch of lantana in the dark is unlikely. You'd have to use torches and cut a path through in some places."

Graham turned the map around to face Jack and Anna. "We've come up with an alternative plan; not sure what you'll think of it."

Anna sat on the ground beside Jack and leaned close. "Whatever it is, we're willing."

Graham nodded. "Good. I'll lead you over the top of the ridge."

"Tonight?" Anna's breathy question echoed Jack's unspoken one.

He met Anna's gaze and the fear in her eyes reminded him. She was afraid of heights. He glanced up to find Graham watching them closely. "How will we see without torches? I'm presuming you don't want lights up on the ridge to alert any watchers?"

"Son, I've been living on this ridge best part of twenty-five years. I never use a torch. Question isn't how will you see, but how well do you trust me?"

Was climbing a steep slope with scree patches and steep drops and no lights a matter of trust? Jack looked at the map again. "It's difficult terrain. No one would expect us to attempt it, let alone do it at night. That's one big positive in its favour. As for trusting you, there's no question of that. But—this proposal is not only dangerous and difficult. Anna's afraid of heights."

Jack was certain Graham felt compassion for Anna, but he kept it out of his expression and his voice. He simply fixed her with his clear gaze.

"Is that right, Anna? So your vote would be to hide in the back of Rick's ute and try that way or attempt to hack a path through the lantana to the creek?"

"You said the car idea probably won't work and the lantana route sounds impossible."

"That's right, but if you can't climb—"

She exhaled a ragged breath. Her chin rose and she met Graham's eyes. "I'll find a way to cope."

"Are you sure?" Jack wasn't certain he masked his concern as well as Graham, but Anna gave him a tremulous smile.

"How could I possibly pass up the chance to be guided by four big brave men?"

Rick grinned. "Three, actually, though I appreciate the compliment. The other part of our plan has me returning home unobserved, making a rather loud exit, courtesy of my loving partner who will explode into a never-before-seen rage to distract the goons stationed on the road near the entrance to the winery. I will proceed to leave some rubber on the road, but will stop to offer assistance to one of the two lookout vehicles. I may offer one of the goons a ride in my car to get help, which should distract them from further thoughts of my vehicle being used to spirit you away."

Graham put a hand on Rick's shoulder. "Rick will drive the

long way around to the other side of the ridge and pick us up there, making certain no one tails him."

Jack nodded. "Sounds good to me. Anna?"

She looked squarely at Graham and Rick. "I trust both of you with my life—with our lives. The ridge it is."

Graham sat back on the log. "Are we all agreed? Kaden, are you happy to try this way, mate?"

Jack realised Kaden had joined them. He hadn't heard the boy's approach. At some point during one of Kaden's visits, he and Graham had nutted out the finer points of moving quietly through the bush.

Anna quickly signed the plan to Kaden, minus Rick's fulsome description. In the back of her mind, she registered that interesting fact. She'd never heard Rick speak at such length, but since he and Geilis had moved in together, the tense man she'd met when Rick first returned to Lark Creek had gone and he was happy.

Kaden nodded and signed a question back to her.

"Right. Kaden asked how will we communicate on the climb tonight if we can't see to sign?"

Graham and Rick looked at each other before Rick rose and went into Graham's tent. He returned with a length of climbing rope, which he looped and tied off around Kaden's waist.

Graham explained with accompanying actions while Anna signed. "You'll be roped together and we'll use a system of distinct tugs. Two tugs means wait for me, I'm having a problem. Three tugs means you've heard something and everyone freezes where they are. Any questions?"

Kaden signed, *What does one tug mean?*

"One tug will mean you've decided to take the express route down the side of the ridge. Try not to use that one, mate." Graham's delivery was deadpan, and it took a moment before Kaden grinned.

Not happening.

"Good. We're all done here. Rick, go set up your distraction and give my apologies to Gei for roping her in.

"Will do. I think she'll get a kick out of helping though, especially since it will give her a chance to yell at me. There's something about make-up sex that—"

Graham held up one hand. "Enough, son, I don't need to hear about it."

Rick was grinning as he shook Jack's hand, kissed Anna's cheek, and then patted Kaden's shoulder. "See you around the far side of the ridge. I'll be the one snoozing in my ute."

"Ute?" Jack had hoped for something less conspicuous, preferably with dark-tinted windows for what he guessed would be a long drive to safety. Dark windows and a warm interior—autumn mornings in Lark Creek were cold and often misty. And they'd be coming off an arduous night climb and descent of O'Reilly's Ridge. "Wait up, could you bring the four-wheel drive?" He glanced at Anna who had her arms wrapped around her waist.

Rick looked at Anna and then at his father.

Graham nodded.

"I'll ask Gei if I can borrow the winery vehicle before we stage our fight. See you folks soon." Rick left quickly and quietly, melting into the bush before Jack could wish him luck.

"Okay, folks, time for a bite to eat and a bit of a rest before it's fully dark. Kaden." Graham touched the teenager's shoulder and looked directly at him as he spoke, using a mixture of mime and speech. "Will you light the gas stove and put the biggest saucepan on it?"

Kaden nodded and headed into the tent, looking pleased to have something to do.

"You're really good with him, Graham." Anna rested her head on Jack's shoulder. He liked the feeling of rightness when she did little things like that; things he would once upon a time have taken for granted. Normal things that from Anna meant so much more.

Jack followed Graham's gaze across his campsite to where Kaden was setting up a single-burner camp stove on a small bottle of gas. He attached the hose with care, as though operating from a mental list of instructions, and it struck Jack that Graham had done much more than point out tree types and wood grain on Kaden's visits.

"He's a good lad, and bright. Reckon he missed out on a lot growing up with an uncle who didn't want him." Graham frowned. "I'll never understand how anyone can ignore a child like that, especially one who had lost both parents the way he did."

There was something in Graham's voice that caught Jack's attention, a wistfulness that reminded him of the lost years sitting between Graham and his son. "It looks like you've taught him a thing or two already, Graham."

"He's a quick learner. I can't work out why Hickman didn't buy him hearing aids and have him taught how to speak. Anna, do you know if there's any medical reason why Kaden can't learn to speak?"

"I don't know, but I'll bet it suited his uncle to have Kaden unable to hear the deals he had going on." Anna had tiptoed around the topic, but Kaden didn't like his uncle and had vented one afternoon.

"He told me his uncle kicked up a stink about sending him to a special school and wouldn't let him have friends visit at home. That's why he went down to the warehouse that day; because he wanted to go away for a weekend with friends from school. I think he's been lonely for a lot of his life."

Graham stood and turned his back on Kaden as he spoke. "That bastard has more than murder to pay for. That boy deserves a chance at a decent life. Have you given any thought to what will happen to the boy once his uncle is in jail?"

Jack shook his head. "We haven't been thinking beyond keeping him safe and just getting through this period."

"Then maybe you need to think about it, sooner rather than

later. There's a good chance Hickman and his crew will be caught by your police friend now they've raised their heads."

Jack slid an arm over Anna's shoulders. "The sooner, the better. Once Hickman is in custody, the state will intervene and put Kaden in foster care. He's only just turned seventeen."

Anna looked up at him. In the late afternoon light, there was a determination in her eyes when she talked about the teenager. "Then we'll start talking about possibilities and come up with a plan, but can we do that once we've got over the ridge? Honestly, I don't think I can focus on something as important as that and follow you along—" She looked up at the towering plug in the centre of the ridge. Her gaze fixed on the steep face and her breathing became shallow.

Jack tried to see it from her perspective. The idea of climbing to the top in daylight was the sort of challenge he would have enjoyed, but at night, with a hearing-impaired teen and a woman afraid of heights—and no lights—

The enormity of the challenge stunned him. He dropped a kiss on her forehead. "You won't see how high it is once we get underway. Graham knows what he's doing. Neither he nor I won't let anything happen to you. Promise."

Chapter 22

Anna helped Kaden wash their bowls and tidy away the remains of their meal. As she dried her hands, her gaze was drawn upwards. Silhouetted against the setting sun the ridge loomed, dark and dangerous over their heads.

She snapped the tea towel and pegged it on the string line running between two small trees. There was too little to do and too much time to think about what lay ahead. Rubbing her hands up her arms did little to warm her, and the light was fading quickly.

Too quickly.

It would be dark soon. She looked up at the ridge towering above them. Would the lack of light hide what she feared, or would her imagination supply what she couldn't see?

Graham and Jack appeared out of the bushes, treading softly. They'd walked to a vantage point to observe what was happening down at her cottage. By their expressions and Jack's finger to his lips, the news couldn't be good.

Anna waited until Jack put an arm around her and voiced her concern. "What did you see?"

"They must have figured we weren't coming back by now. Graham saw one of them finally notice the cameras on the house, and a couple of them came out from inside. The monitors in your room will confirm we had advance warning they were on their way."

"So, does that affect our plans?"

"Maybe. Rory called me while we were watching the cottage to ask what was going on and were we in some sort of trouble because a couple of Hickman's men had called in to the farm. They were flashing a photo of Kaden and claiming he'd run away from his uncle."

"That's true, but not the whole story. What did he tell them?"

"Only that Kaden had been caught stealing and he'd turned the boy over to the police. It seems he was suspicious enough of them not to mention the sudden appearance of your *deaf brother*."

Graham joined them with Kaden and looked at Jack. "Have you told her?"

Jack's arm tightened around her shoulders. "Most of it. Graham thinks we should make our way to the edge of the bush below the ridge now."

"You mean to start climbing in the light?" Her breath stuck in her throat. Would it be worse to see the drop, or to imagine it?

"No. We'll wait just inside the tree line for full dark. Moonrise is late tonight. So long as we get to that spot on the right shoulder of the plug—" He pointed out a narrow gap before a steep drop. "We'll be over the other side before the moonlight gives us away."

"Why the urgency now?"

The men exchanged a glance and Graham nodded. "You tell her. I'll get the packs."

Jack took hold of both her shoulders. In the fast disappearing light, she was shocked to see the worry in his eyes. "We spotted movement heading up the fence line of the Donovan farm. We think they've started searching the surrounding area for you and Kaden."

She pressed her lips together, holding in frustration and fear and the desire to scream at fate. Two deep breaths later she couldn't still her pounding heart, but she looked at him. "Let's get going."

Graham handed each of them a pack, reserving the heavier food and water and two lengths of climbing rope for himself. "From now on, not a word. Do your best to tread lightly. Try not to kick any loose stones over the edge. I'll tie the ropes on when we reach the tree line. Two tugs means what?" He looked at Kaden, tugged the rope twice and raised an eyebrow.

Wait for me, I need help.

Graham nodded. "And what does three mean, Anna?"

"I've heard or seen something and everyone freezes where they are."

"Good. Let's go."

They followed close behind Graham through bushes and small trees clinging in soil that became stonier as they climbed. The slope increased, gradually at first, but by the time Graham signalled a halt, Anna had turned sideways and was digging in with the toes and sides of her boots.

Silently, Graham lowered his gear to the ground, except for a rope, which he unwound and knotted around her waist. He leaned close and whispered, "Not too tight?"

"It's fine," she whispered back.

He moved on, connecting Kaden and then Jack, keeping Kaden between her and Jack. Anna could barely see Graham now. In his dark clothing he was no more than a shadow against the midnight blue of the sky. She felt a light pull as he attached the rope around his waist and then nothing.

Waiting for full dark to fall, nerves kicked in. Her breathing sounded loud in her ears; her heart thundered as she saw in her mind's eye the bulk and steeply sloping ridge that lay ahead. How could they scale it in the dark?

Graham's hand gripped her shoulder and squeezed before he gently drew her forwards. The rope guided her direction, and she concentrated on placing her feet carefully, feeling the ground ahead before she let her weight down on her leading foot. It made for slow going, but it also distracted her from thoughts of the open air on her right side.

As they climbed, she tuned her focus onto Graham, listening for each tiny sound, a scrape of boot on stone, the brush of the backpack against the rock face. And always they moved upwards. Sometimes the slope was gentle for a few metres, and sometimes Graham hauled her up and over a section more suited to a mountain goat than to man. When he finally paused, Anna pressed back against the solid face of rock. The lights of Lark Creek twinkled in the distance. It felt as thought they were on a relatively flat ledge—flat, but narrow as she discovered when she felt the ground in front of her. The toe of her boot dropped into thin air no more than a body width in front of her.

Beside her, Kaden pulled himself up with a soft grunt. The gentle slackening of the rope against her leg guided her as she reached down to help him. A boot scrabbled against rock before he turned around and sat on the edge of the ledge, breathing heavily.

Below she could just hear Jack's progress on the boulder Graham had hauled her over. Pressed back against the face of the ridge, she listened for the sounds of him approaching the ledge.

The brief respite was welcome. Thigh muscles unused to climbing ached and quivered as she leaned against the rock in the darkness. She fixed her gaze on the town beyond the trees on the lower slopes of the ridge. From this height, it was small and peaceful and so far away. Tracing the line of lights along Main Street to where it curved just past the police station, she saw the pattern of streets laid out.

How high they had already climbed because a murderer and his band of thugs were chasing them. Funny how the fear of death at their hands spurred her on to face one of her biggest phobias.

But what if they found Graham's campsite and noticed the recent evidence of several people having been there? Were they following them even now?

Anna strained her ears to listen for sounds of pursuit.

Not far below where she could hear Jack clambering over the boulder, a pinprick of light flickered and vanished. She peered into the blackness of the bush stretching between the ridge and the lights of town. The light failed to reappear.

Longing for reassurance and knowing she must not say a word, she tried to catch a glimpse of Jack. He'd been right about the darkness hiding what she feared, but it also hid him from her sight.

The sound of a boot slipping on rock rose from below.

She leaned forward, keeping hold of a knob of rock behind her. Jack was there, somewhere in the black void. If only she could see him. And suddenly there was a light bobbing erratically along the route she thought they had taken.

Her breathing froze on a gasp. Nerveless fingers slipped from the rock. *Close enough to be Ferdy's men pursuing them . . . and Jack was down there!*

She tugged the ropes connecting her to Graham and Kaden three times and willed Kaden to pass it on to Jack.

In the dark landscape, sounds magnified and carried up the slope. A slippage of boots on the scree patch, a quickly cut off swear word. How many of Hickman's men were following them? How far did they have to climb to reach the gap Graham had pointed out?

Conscious of her breathing, loud in her ears, she tried to draw shallow breaths. Willing the men following them to stop and turn back, she bit back a cry of fear as a bright beam of light began a sweep over the ridge.

Graham pushed her down until she sprawled in the dirt and reached past her to Kaden. She heard the swish of dirt and felt his warm breath on her arm as he dropped onto the ledge and lay still. The torchlight passed above their heads where, moments earlier, they'd been standing.

Anna shoved her knuckle in her mouth, tasting dirt as she suppressed a whimper. Now was not the time to have a meltdown. If their pursuers decided to follow them, their torches gave them a huge advantage in covering ground quickly. But why would they consider the ridge as an escape route? Was it possible someone had inadvertently given them away?

She tracked the torch beam as it climbed higher, all the way to the top of the ridge before dropping quickly. Maybe they would be okay. Dare she hope?

"What's that?" The question was accompanied by the torchlight zeroing in on a point not far below them. A halo of light spilled over the lip of the ledge.

From behind her, she heard a soft "shit" from Graham. He touched her leg and crawled carefully up beside her until his head was near her waist.

His whisper was harsh. "They've spotted the rope. Cut it between Jack and Kaden." The handle of a knife pressed into her hand.

Cut Jack's rope? Cast him adrift on the steep side of the ridge so they could escape . . .

"Do it now or we're all dead." Low as Graham's voice was it carried an air of command that forced her into action.

She crawled towards Kaden, patted his shoulder, and, reaching down to his waist, sawed through the rope attaching the teenager to Jack. As the rope slipped through her fingers, she felt twin trails of moisture running down her cheeks.

A moment later, the soft thud of rope landing on the boulder below was accompanied by Jack standing and waving his arms at the men with the torch.

"Hoi there! Help."

Anna peeked over the edge and her heart thudded to a different beat. The light shone squarely on Jack who was now in plain sight of their pursuers.

"I had a bit of a fall. Can you help me get down?"

"Who are you, and what are you doing up there at night?" At the edge of the torch beam, Anna could just make out what looked like a gun slung over the second man's shoulder as he edged up beside the man holding the torch.

"Name's Jack. I'm new to the town. Someone told me the sunset view from up here was spectacular, but they didn't tell me how dangerous it was. I slipped and caught my rope on a rock or something. I've just worked it free. Any chance you can light my way down to you?"

"Sure, come on down. See anyone else up there?" The light played up and over the rock face above them and Anna pressed into the ledge.

"Mate, you're kidding. No one could climb this insane chunk of rock at night. Thought I was stuck on that boulder until daylight."

The beam of light continued along the upper section of the ridge before dropping and lighting Jack's way down to the two men.

As Jack eased back off the boulder, Anna noticed he was limping. Was it genuine or part of his cover story? It seemed to take forever for him to reach the men below and when he did, they kept the torch fixed on his face. *Hiding their identity?*

Graham waited until the torchlight and the men disappeared into the bush before tapping her calf. In a daze of disbelief, she tapped Kaden and the two of them edged forwards, blindly following Graham upwards until they stepped through a narrow split in the rock. Behind them, just breaching the horizon, a waning moon appeared, bathing the landscape on the eastern side of O'Reilly's Ridge in moonlight. A sliver of light cut through the split they had traversed, catching a reflective strip on Kaden's hoodie.

Graham pulled him out of the moonlight and patted his shoulder. "We made it just in time."

"Thanks to Jack sacrificing himself. But he's in danger. Graham, they've got Jack."

"If he keeps his head, he'll be okay." Graham checked the short piece of rope hanging from Kaden's waist. He wrapped it once more around him and tucked the cut end in.

"You don't sound certain."

Graham checked the knots attaching Anna to Kaden, and

those tethering her to him as he replied. "There's nothing to link him to you unless Hickman's men have spoken to people in town yet. Jack figured that out and he's chosen to be a decoy, like Rick. He's given you a chance to get away. Use it well."

"But what if—"

"Anna, it won't help to think of ifs and buts now. We work with what we've got. Do you need a moment to catch your breath, or shall we keep heading towards Rick and the car?"

Anna tipped her head up to the sky, seeing the Southern Cross low on the horizon. She wanted time with Jack to lie out under those stars and pick out other constellations. Time to get to know him better; time to let these feelings for him resolve themselves into what she suspected just might be love. He'd given them a chance by the choice he'd made. She refused to waste it.

"Jack's a big boy. He's given us this chance so let's get Kaden away to safety."

***

Aware that the men had deliberately blinded him with the torchlight, Jack played along. Any extra time he could create for Graham to get Anna and Kaden away from Lark Creek was a bonus. Smithy would arrange somewhere safe for them—new names, new home, probably somewhere far away.

Even if it meant he'd never see Anna again, he'd take the same actions to ensure she was safe. That they were safe.

Not just because it was the right thing to do, but because he loved her so much. Enough to let her go.

Tamping down the wrenching sense of loss, he limped slowly ahead in the torchlight. "I can't thank you guys enough. If you hadn't come along when you did I'd have had a really uncomfortable night. Cold too. Who were you looking for up there?" He stabbed a thumb back the way they'd come.

"Our boss's nephew has gone missing. He's worried the boy's been kidnapped." Jack identified the voice as belonging to the torch holder. If he could keep them talking, maybe he'd have enough to identify their voices later.

The second man added, "Yeah, by a woman—blonde-haired. See anyone like that around here?"

"Mate, if I'd seen a woman like that up there, I wouldn't have been so keen to get down off the damned ridge." The irony was that he hadn't been able to see Anna when they were climbing. His last memory of her would be her smile as she bravely agreed to the climb.

They continued down the trail with little more to say. The going got easier when the path flattened out and merged with the track that led across the top of the Donovan farm.

"So, where's your car parked, mate?" The torch carrier was close behind and the hair on Jack's neck stood on end.

"I left it at the winery. I bought some of their wine and they agreed to let me leave it parked there while I climbed the ridge to look at the sunset." Thinking furiously, Jack realised it was likely the men in Anna's cottage would have spotted his gear, maybe even got his name from one of the files sitting on top of his pile of bedding. If that were the case, heading back to the cottage would be walking into a shitload of trouble.

He pointed vaguely in the direction of the Donovan farmhouse. "I might call in and see if these folks can strap my ankle. It's giving me curry. Thanks for your help, guys. Appreciate it."

Torch man put a hand on Jack's shoulder. "I tell you what, how about you come back to—our place. We'll fix your ankle there."

"I don't want to put you to any more trouble on my account."

"No trouble, mate. It's just through this gate." The hand on his shoulder applied enough pressure that Jack knew better than to try to evade them. He'd seen the outline of a gun before the second man had tucked it against his side. Making a stupid move might attract Rory or his father into danger and that wasn't an option.

Jack couldn't think how to avoid going with them without making a scene. Hoping Graham had had enough time to get Anna and Kaden off the ridge and down to Rick's car, he slowed his pace a little more. Once these men realised his ankle wasn't injured, who knew what they might decide to do?

Where are you, Smithy? We need the cavalry now.

As they turned around Anna's garden shed, the house was a blaze of lights. The dark grey hulk of the gang's SUV sat between the cottage and the fire pit. Twin pinpricks of glowing cigarettes placed two of Hickman's men beside the fire pit. Shadowy figures crossed behind curtained windows inside the cottage. How many were there? If he could assess the situation and get the information to Smithy, maybe he could take most of the gang into custody. If they got all of Hickman's gang, maybe Anna and Kaden wouldn't have to go into hiding.

It was dangerous letting his attention stray into maybe territory.

"After you." Torch man pointed the way with his torch and Jack reluctantly hobbled up the back stairs.

Three men lounged against the sink and kitchen cupboards. A man of average height, but portly, was seated at Anna's table. He had something of the look of Kaden about him, but with a sharp edge in his gaze. It had to be Hickman. He glanced past Jack and focussed on the man holding the torch. "I sent you to find my nephew and the woman and you bring me a man. Why?"

"We found him near the top of that ridge, boss. Said he'd fallen and his rope was caught on rocks. We spotted the rope and watched it come loose."

Hickman turned to Jack. "Tell me, *friend*, what you were doing up on that ridge at this time of night." The voice was almost friendly, but the undertone sent a chill down Jack's spine. This wasn't a man to get on the wrong side of.

"As I told the other bloke, I'm new to town. Someone told me I should check out the sunset from up on the ridge, but I slipped and my rope caught in rocks. I injured my ankle and figured I was stuck there for the night."

"Who goes climbing in a place like that in the dark, without a torch?"

"Lost it when I fell. And it wasn't dark when I started back down."

Stay consistent as far as possible. Stick as close to the truth as you can so you don't get caught out.

"Hmm, and you didn't see my nephew or a woman up that way?" The eyes narrowed as Hickman looked Jack up and down before settling on his face.

"No. I was really glad when these two boys turned up."

"And that rope around your shoulder, that's the one you were using?"

Jack patted the rope he'd coiled and carried down off the ridge. "Thought it might be useful. It's pretty steep up there. I should have paid more attention to the folks who warned me against trying the climb than the guy who suggested I do it. Plenty of folks think the area is haunted. I must say, I was beginning to imagine the ghost of someone who'd fallen to their death while I was stuck on that boulder. Look, I don't want to hold up your search for your nephew. My car's over in the winery car park so—"

Hickman held out his hand and gave a smile that was all white teeth and menace. "Show me your rope."

Thoughts of scoping the situation and texting information to Smithy evaporated as Jack handed over the coiled rope. One end was neatly finished, shop-new and undistinguished. The other end, the one that risked giving him away, had been roughly hacked by an inexpert hand with a knife.

When Hickman saw those cuts he'd guess the rest.

And Jack's life wouldn't be worth Jack shit.

Chapter 23

Anna spotted a glint as moonlight touched metal beneath a tree on the rough track. She touched Graham's shoulder, pointed, and whispered. "Is that Rick's car?"

Graham nodded. "Yes. Stay here. I'll do a reccy first."

Anna put a hand out to prevent Kaden following and pulled him back into the deepest shadow, holding her breath as Graham disappeared, incredibly grateful for his survival skills and bushcraft that had brought them this far. Her senses were ratcheted up so high, she could rival Spiderman right now.

A faint crackle of leaves behind them had her turn to face whatever was out there. As she pushed Kaden down into a crouch, her free hand felt around for a stone or a branch, anything she could use for defence. Her fingers closed around a chunk of rock. Raising her arm, she tried to quiet her breathing before a shadow stopped in front of her. She sensed the man as she gripped the rock and moved her arm back for a solid thwack.

The shadow spoke softly, in a voice that was familiar and welcome. "Anna, it's Rick."

Her hand dropped as she stood slowly, peering into the darkness. "Your father went to check the car."

"We met up. All clear this side of the ridge. Come on." She reached for Kaden and tugged him upright, pulling him along beside her.

The back door of the car was opened as they neared the vehicle, but the only light that showed was one built low into the door frame. Graham stood with one hand out. "Give me your backpacks. I'll put them in the boot. You can bring your rock if you want to, Anna." She couldn't see his face, but his voice held compassion.

Anna looked down, surprised to see she still held her weapon. With a conscious effort, she willed her fingers to unclench. The rock dropped with a soft thud into the dirt and she handed over her backpack before climbing into the car. As she shuffled across to the other side and reached for the seatbelt, a tremor passed through her. The hours since Jack had first spotted Hickman's men approaching felt like a bad dream. Their escape up the ridge in the black of night, and Jack's heroic diversion replayed as the boot shut with a soft thud and the others clambered into the car.

Was Smithy nearby with a back up force or would Hickman get away before reinforcements arrived? And if that happened, would she ever see Jack again?

Rick started the engine and eased the SUV onto the track. They ran dark and slow until the dirt track met up with a single lane of country back road. Only then did Rick turn on the headlights and increase speed.

Anna looked through the side window. When she spotted the Southern Cross and the Pointers glowing brightly, she realised they were heading north.

Away from Lark Creek—where she'd run to find healing. Where she'd found Jack.

***

Jack slumped in the kitchen chair, hands tied behind him and the top corners of the chair digging into his armpits. His headache thumped with an urgency that had everything to do with keeping his wits about him as Hickman's men grilled him. Hickman himself sat directly opposite Jack, sipping a coffee. The smell turned Jack's stomach while his dry mouth thirsted for water.

"Jack, it will go so much better for you if you simply tell us where my nephew is."

A snake hissing. That's what Hickman's voice reminded him of. A snake in the grass, lethal, poised to strike.

And if Jack didn't concentrate and stick with his story, if he slipped up, Hickman would get his hands on Jack's family. The slide of blood down his cheek reminded him what was at stake and who he was up against. "I told you why I was up on the ridge." He tipped his head back and peered at the gangland boss through narrowed eyes. Anna's kitchen lights had always struck him as dim before, but now, they seemed as bright as the sun.

"Yeah, looking at sunsets. Funny but you don't strike me as a sunset kind of guy."

"What do you want me say?"

Hickman thumped the table. "Where is Kaden?"

Jack shook his head and instantly regretted the movement. "Don't know any Kaden."

"Boss? You need to see this." One of the men, who looked more intelligent than the others, presented his phone to Hickman.

"What is it?"

"Police report from a few days after the boy disappeared. It just came through. Check out the name of the duty solicitor. And then check the name on this file." He dropped Jack's blue conveyancing file onto the table. "Found it in the corner of the lounge room down the side of a pile of bedding."

How did they access confidential police reports? Kaden's comment about important people niggled at the edge of Jack's mind. Hickman had paid off the right people so he had to have access to someone in Brisbane. Someone high enough up the food chain to get around confidentiality blocks.

Hickman looked at the screen, at the file, and then at Jack. "Where are my nephew and the woman, and don't insult me by claiming you don't know them. Your file is in Anna Wilkins' house."

No matter what answer he gave, he was screwed.

Come on, Smithy. Where's the cavalry when you need them?

Jack shrugged, certain he wasn't going to get out of the

cottage alive, and tried to fix an image in his mind, of Anna and Kaden safely down the other side of the ridge and far away from the reach of Kaden's uncle.

Hickman stood and held out his hand. The other man took back his phone and placed the butt of his gun in his boss' hand.

The click of the safety being flicked off was loud in the quiet of the kitchen. Hickman walked around the table, his leather boots squeaking with each step. "One more time, *Mister Donaldson.* Tell me where they are."

"I can't tell you what I don't know." Jack gritted his teeth. He knew what came next.

Hickman raised his gun arm and stepped towards him.

***

"Anna." The voice came from far away. Tired and with muscles she didn't know she had protesting their ill-usage, she tried to roll over and turn away, but something stopped her moving. Suddenly the constriction disappeared and someone shook her shoulder.

"Jack?" From the depths of her bad dream, she swam towards the surface, forcing her gritty eyes open.

"It's Graham. Jack's not here, love. Come on, we're at our next stop."

She blinked and tried to collect her scattered wits. *Jack's not here. Then where is he?*

Graham moved back and Smithy stepped up and held out a hand. "I'll take you and Jed to your next safe house."

"We can't go. Jack's not here." Anna sat up. She was in the back of Rick's car and one arm was caught in the seatbelt and . . . the memory slammed into her like a B-double truck.

Jack hadn't made it out.

His absence sucked all the light and warmth from around her. She pressed her lips together. "Jack tried to throw them off our trail. Do you know if—"

"I'm sorry, Anna. I don't have any information about him

yet. We have to go. Thanks to Graham and Rick you two are safe. That's all I can tell you for now." Smithy's hand remained in her sight as he waited for her to accept the next stage of their flight from Kaden's uncle.

As if she had a choice. She wanted to tell them to take her back to the ridge. If she had to climb the damned chunk of rock again to find Jack so they could be together, she'd do it in a heartbeat. But Jack's actions had always shown him for the decent man he was. And his actions last night had been deliberate. He'd known his choice to let her go was the only way she could leave. He'd let her go without him. Jack trusted Smithy to see her and Kaden safe; she could do no less.

She accepted the offer of Smithy's hand, stepped out of Rick's car and turned to Graham. "Thanks for all you and Rick have done. Please—tell Jack for me that—" Her throat closed around words she wanted to say to him. Words she promised herself she would say to his face one day.

"I'll tell him, but I reckon he knows, lass. Stay safe."

She reached up and kissed his cheek, then turned quickly away so he wouldn't see the tears pricking her eyes. Kaden was standing beside a black four-wheel drive parked in front of Rick's. Heavily tinted windows made her feel as though she was in some bizarre B-grade thriller. As she approached, Kaden opened a door for her. She climbed in without a backward glance.

There was no use looking back. No point regretting what she hadn't said to Jack. Fate had stepped in and separated them. Now it was up to her to accept Smithy's course that led to safety for her and for Kaden.

Chapter 24

Dust tickled Jack's nose. He didn't like dust. It made him sneeze. He much preferred Anna's scent, and her body spooning with his. *'S funny, I never liked sleeping like that with anyone before Anna.* He turned his head.

Pain shot from the base of his skull and consumed his ability to think. Gently he turned his head to the side. The pain eased a little, but purple shooting stars filled his vision. He tried to lift his hand to feel his head. Rope held both wrists tightly together and led down to his ankles. Now he thought about it he wasn't sure which pain was worse—his head, or the pain shooting like flames from his screaming shoulders. When he tried to move, the rope seemed to tighten—or was that his body protesting being trussed up like a turkey dinner?

Opening aching eyes—*was there any part of him that wasn't aching?* —he noticed thin daylight seeping through a crack in a door. Except the door seemed to be above him.

"Anyone there?" Had he made a sound? He added his parched throat to the list of aching body parts, cleared it and tried calling again. "Hello?"

Where the hell am I?

Accepting he was alive for now, he tried to stay calm and learn more about his immediate environment. Widening his eyes, he gingerly turned his head, stopping short of putting pressure on what felt like an emu egg on the back of his skull. Undressed timber walls seemed to enclose him. The floor beneath smelled like earth so maybe the door was in fact a trapdoor.

Having established some sort of orientation, he pulled his knees towards his chest and rolled up onto them. Waves of nausea pulsed through his stomach. He rode out the worst of the pain before lifting his head. Something about the floorboards above seemed familiar. Wide and with occasional knotty points, they looked like . . . His head pounded and he tried to concentrate. Where had he seen boards like that?

Stealthy footfalls passed over his head, treading carefully.

"Clear, lounge room."

"Clear bedroom one . . . bedroom two . . . bathroom . . ."

"No sign of the missing man. It looks like they cleared out in a hurry."

" . . .on their way back to Brisbane . . . Polair . . . second team will intercept them."

Fragments of a conversation drifted with dust motes on the air. Were Smithy's men above? There was only one way to find out.

"Hello, anybody up there?" Jack's voice rasped like a rough woodwork file.

Booted feet, no longer attempting caution, dislodged more dust. They stopped above him. "There." Hinges squeaked.

Light streamed in, beautiful, blinding light.

"Sir, we've found him. He's alive."

##

Jack downed his second glass of water before the medic wrapped a bandage around his wrist. The antiseptic spray had stung and he'd hissed in a breath.

The medic, a young woman, grinned. "Swear if it helps. I've heard it all before." She placed an adhesive strip across the end of the bandage, turned back to her kit and opened another sealed packet.

Jack exhaled slowly. "It's fine. You're doing a great job."

"Well done, Jack." She smiled and gave his other wrist similar treatment. Added to the bandage around his head, the latest one made him feel like an extra on the set of a zombie horror film. The glimpse he'd caught of himself in the bathroom mirror once the special police team had freed him from the wood cellar showed he'd be well cast as a zombie. Dried blood and dark bruises would frighten little children. He dreaded to think what Anna would say when . . .

His gut clenched as a different sort of pain consumed him. Would he see her again or would the case against Ferdy Hickman take a couple of years to build? Until the gang boss was behind bars, Anna and Kaden wouldn't be able to live a normal life—one that he had hoped to be part of.

"Any chance I can borrow a phone? I want to call Smithy."

The special police team member assigned to accompany him looked blank. "Who?"

"Charles Smith, the bloke in charge of this little shindig."

"Gotcha. No can do. He's on assignment. No contact until he's completed it. Sorry, sir."

Jack looked down at the empty glass in his hand. *Of course he is. He wouldn't trust this task to anyone else.*

It should have made Jack feel better.

He doubted anything but the sight of Anna walking back to him would ever make him feel better again.

***

Anna turned a full circle and looked around the townhouse. *Their safe house for the next however long.*

On the outside there was nothing to distinguish it from its neighbours other than security screens on doors that Anna feared would keep out the flies and little else. Second floor, two bedrooms, a small kitchen, lounge-dining area, one bathroom. Not so different from her cottage, minus the charm.

"I know it doesn't look like much, but—"

"It's fine, Smithy, thanks. Can we go out for supplies? How does this whole thing work?"

Kaden slumped on the couch and closed his eyes.

Smithy drew Anna behind the couch and kneeled beside a rug. He flicked the corner back and lifted an inset silver pull, revealing a trapdoor in the floor. "This leads into the apartment below, where two of our agents will be stationed. I'll introduce them when they arrive in the next hour or so. You have three choices of exit—front, back or floor should the need arise. I don't expect it will."

"Need? As in if Hickman traces us here? How likely is that?"

"Unless someone else posts a picture of you and *your brother* again, not likely, but try not to go to anything that smacks of being social." Smithy stood and dropped the rug back over the trapdoor.

Anna grabbed the back of the sofa and hauled herself upright. Fatigue had set in and her leg muscles trembled. "Right. And food?"

"Basics in fridge and pantry. Anything else you need or want, text the guys downstairs. Your story is that you and your brother have just lost your parents. No one will expect you to be very sociable under those circumstances. And your names are now Hannah and Michael Renshaw. If anyone searches the name, they'll find a middle-aged couple from Sydney, recently deceased in an accident on a highway."

She wrapped her arms around her waist and glanced at the sleeping teenager. "Is that a fair cover story to inflict on Kaden? That's what happened to his parents."

"That's what he believes happened to them. In fact his father was killed in a gangland type execution and his mother came home early."

Anna's empty stomach churned. She closed her eyes and leaned against the sofa, her fingers digging into the cushioned top as Smithy continued.

"Hickman killed his brother-in-law and his own sister. There wasn't enough evidence to pin it on him."

When she opened her eyes, Smithy was watching her carefully. "Now do you understand why he won't think twice about getting rid of his nephew? Why it's imperative that you don't draw any attention to yourselves?"

Not trusting her voice she nodded, a jerk of the head like a puppet on a string.

"I'm sorry you were thrust into this mess, Anna, but I know you have the mental strength to cope. Anyone brave enough to take on a traumatised teenager as you have and tackle that ridge in the dark is tops in my book. I know Jack thinks I'm an insensitive and ungrateful bastard at times but believe me–I do understand how hard this is on you, and I'm glad Kaden has you on his side."

Compliments usually went over Anna's head, but Smithy's touched something deep in her. Maybe because he was who he was, it meant more than any other. "Thank you. I'll do my best for him."

"I know."

She looked through the window at a flat landscape, different and drier than that of Lark Creek. What would they do to keep themselves occupied here in—wherever they were? Her backpack contained a change of clothes, a travel pack of toiletries, and not so much as a notebook and pencil. *I'll go crazy if I can't go out.* "Any chance of getting me some art supplies too? Even a sketch book and pencils would do."

Smithy nodded. "Not a problem, but it would be better if you didn't mention your art to anyone. Hannah needs to be in a solitary type of occupation but as different from an artist as you can make her."

"Something online maybe? A coder?"

"Sure, just make sure everything you do from now on is as Hannah Renshaw, got it?" When she nodded, Smithy took out a notebook and basic mobile phone and handed both to her. "Email account is already set up in your new name. Passwords are in here, along with my contact number and the number for the guys downstairs. But Anna, you can't contact Jack, not under any circumstances."

Her gaze rose to meet Smithy's before flinching away from the understanding in his eyes. "I know."

Outside, the sky was overcast and the scent of rain drifted through the narrow opening in one window.

"How about I make us a coffee while you have a look in the bedrooms and bathroom. Check to see if you have all you need for the next few days and then we'll go over the ground rules with Kaden." Smithy glanced at the sleeping teenager. "I guess there's one advantage to not being able to hear—bet he can sleep anywhere."

"Probably. Help yourself to whatever's in the cupboard. I'll be back in a couple of minutes."

"Take all the time you need. I'm not going anywhere until you've got what you need."

Anna walked into the back bedroom and closed the door. What she needed was to get back to Jack and that was the one thing Smithy wouldn't—couldn't give her.

By the time she'd looked through the basic clothes and toiletries provided for her and for Kaden, the kettle was whistling in the kitchen and a double knock sounded from the front door. Closing the mirrored bathroom cabinet, she caught sight of her face for the first time in almost twenty-four hours. Red eyes, dark shadows and yesterday's flaking mascara peered tiredly back from the image in the mirror.

Checking there was a towel on the railing, she turned on the cold tap and splashed water over her face. When Smithy left, she'd curl up and try to sleep. When Smithy was gone . . .

Her last link with Jack moved quietly around in the kitchen making coffee. The crinkle of packaging being opened was followed by Smithy calling to her. "Coffee's ready and food if you're hungry."

She shook water from her hands and patted her face on the towel. A quick glance at the woman in the mirror showed a little improvement in her appearance. It would have to do. "Coming."

On the small square dining table three mugs of coffee sent steam lazily spiralling into the air. Huddled together in the centre of the table, three buckets of takeaway noodles stood beside three sets of chopsticks.

"Ted and Hugo, your guardians, arrived and dropped off a meal. They're setting up downstairs while we eat. Take your pick. There's beef with black bean, chicken chow mien, and a vegetarian one with tofu."

"Any of those will suit me. You choose." She touched Kaden on the shoulder and, when he opened heavy-lidded eyes, signed, *Food on the table.*

He stretched and yawned before bouncing to his feet and dropping into the nearest chair. With a quick glance at Smithy and Anna, he reached for the bucket of beef noodles.

Smithy shrugged and drew the bucket of chicken in front of him.

The scent of chow mien hit Anna and she swallowed against the bile rising in her throat. She didn't care which meal she got. Chances were she'd eat a token mouthful and put the rest in the fridge. As she fiddled with her chopsticks and delayed eating, an idea took up residence in her mind and wouldn't leave. Chopsticks poised above her meal, she pinned Smithy with a look she tried not to let appear as desperate as she felt. "Will you take a note to Jack from me? I promise I won't mention where I am, or anything about what happened, but I need to tell him something. Please? This is my last chance to communicate with Jack, maybe for a very long time."

***

"Glad to see you looking so good, mate." Smithy stuck out a hand and Jack shook it.

"Yeah, I should look this good all the time." Bandaged and bruised, he'd opted to work from home for the next few days and have Moira drop files in to him. Moira would be discreet and he didn't want his battered appearance to raise more questions about

Anna and Kaden's sudden disappearance. "Come in. Coffee?"

Wishing he'd been able to return to the cottage and sleep in the bed that still held the scent of Anna, even hold the pillow she slept on, instead, he was back in his rented house in town. He'd wanted to be surrounded by her art; to feel her essence around him. Not to be stuck in this empty, echoing house.

Black-dusted fingerprints and white-suited forensic officers had filled her cottage. Surreptitiously, he wiped his hands on his jeans. Even with modern technology the experience of being digitally fingerprinted so officers could identify his prints from Hickman's men left him feeling tainted.

"Coffee, yeah thanks." Smithy followed him into the kitchen.

"Fancy a slug of something in it, or would that go against your no drinking on the job policy?"

"Sure, I'll join you." He took out a notebook and Jack turned away to fill the kettle. "How are you really doing, mate? Didn't fancy a couple of nights in hospital?"

"I'm okay." Smithy's concern was unexpected, not least because he never let the personal into his working life. But they'd been friends for a long time. Jack felt Smithy's piercing gaze slice him open like a scalpel. "How would you expect me to be?"

"Thought you might be missing Anna."

Trust his friend to cut to the heart of the matter, but neither of them did the *talking about feelings* stuff. Ever.

Jack paused with the teaspoon deep in the coffee jar and turned. "Smithy, you're freaking me out. Since when have you become a relationship advisor?"

"Since my best mate fell for the woman he involved in my current case. We need to do a full interview when you're up to it, but I dropped by on a purely personal call."

"I'm fine to answer any questions you've got right now." Interrogation was preferable to discussion of his love life. He finished making the coffee and set two mugs on the table before picking up a bottle of spiced rum. "Will this do?"

"Yeah. So you're fine to accompany me to our temporary incident room today?"

"Like I said, I'm good to go." Jack dropped onto the seat across from Smithy's and sipped his coffee. Hot, black and spiked to dull the pain of loss. Not that anything short of Anna's return would ease his missing her.

Smithy reached into the inside pocket of his jacket and withdrew a folded piece of paper, ragged-edged where it had been torn out of a spiral-bound notebook. He slid the paper across the table, picked up his mug of coffee and stood. "I'm just going to look at the view from your front veranda. Join me when you're ready." He strolled through the door leaving Jack staring after him.

Who was that and what has he done with my friend?

Jack closed his eyes on the inane thought. Maybe his concussion was giving him delusions. He set the mug down. A little liquid slopped onto the paper Smithy had dropped onto the table.

Jack picked it up and shook off the drops of coffee. He reached behind him for the dishcloth and wiped away the rest. Why hadn't his friend said anything about the paper? Why toss it on the table and leave before—

He turned the note over as though it might bite. Blank on the outside, the thin paper held ridged impressions of letters where a pen had pressed too hard.

Slowly, Jack opened the note. Familiar handwriting in sky-blue ink covered the page—right slanting, with artistic swirls on letters that dipped below the faint blue lines of the paper. His gaze dropped to the signature.

Anna.

Bless Smithy for his discretion and his sudden interest in Jack's personal life. And his discretion in disappearing while Jack read her letter. Jack drank a mouthful of coffee before settling back to read Anna's note.

My darling,

I promised I'd say only what was necessary. It's this: I love you.

I know it seems crazy after such a short time, but there it is. I feel like I imagine my grandmother felt when she met and married her sailor within three short, but intense weeks. She always said war (and by that I think she meant any situation where you don't know if you'll live to see another day) sharpens the senses and shortens the usual time frames society expects relationships to follow.

I don't know if you feel the same. It may not matter, but I wanted you to know, especially as I was so awful to you when we met. You've shown me in a thousand ways that you're a good man, and I can trust you with everything I am.

I can't regret the time we shared. I've never been one for blind faith, but there is a part of me that believes you'll find some way back to me.

I love you.

A xx

Chapter 25

"Hello, Jack, good to see you out and about. Heard from Moira that you had a bad dose of the flu." Rhoda Alexopoulos beamed at him over the counter of her takeaway enterprise. "I have made *gyros* tonight and there are little tubs of *tzatziki* and pita bread to wrap around the meat. So three serves for you?"

"Ah, just one serve thanks, Rhoda."

She clicked her tongue and shook her head. "So it's true then. Anna and Jed have gone. I'm sorry." She added a comment in Greek that, by her tone, Jack figured meant something like *poor man*.

"It's okay, Rhoda. I'm really missing them, but Anna's going to stay with Jed while he's fitted with some new type of hearing aid." If he stuck with Smithy's version of the story, he could almost believe it was possible to pick up the phone and call Anna, and hear her laughter and her love filter through the connection.

Rhoda's expression brightened. "Ah, she's not *gone*-gone, just away. That's a good thing, isn't it? But it's hard when your loved ones are far away." Rhoda slipped two pieces of pita bread into a brown paper bag and added a small plastic tub of sauce. She set them on top of the container of lamb. "You want I should keep a serve of dinner for you each night we're open? Just until Anna gets back."

"That would be great, thanks. Until Anna gets back."

The words repeated in his mind as he walked the length of Main Street with his bag of takeaway and turned down his street. They stayed with him as he sat in front of the television with his dinner.

The ABC news introduction played as he added *tzatziki* over the meat on the pita bread. A blob dripped onto his thumb. He licked it off and reached for a paper serviette as the first story began. Perhaps that was why he missed seeing the headline.

"A successful police raid on premises in Brisbane has netted a pile of drugs, weapons and one of Australia's most wanted criminals. Ferdinand Hickman and most of his gang were caught when . . ." Jack set aside the dinner tray and grabbed the remote, turning the volume up.

"Until Anna comes home." Jack spoke the words aloud. They hung in the dim lounge room like a promise, like the first step of the journey that would bring Anna home. *To him.*

##

Jack gripped his mobile as his call to Smithy connected.

"I'm guessing you heard it on the news." Smithy sounded elated, an unfamiliar state for his phlegmatic friend.

"It's good news, right? It means you'll be able to bring them home at some point."

"Hold your horses, Jack. You should know better than most how long some cases take to put together."

"I know, but—"

"I'm crossing every T and dotting every I. Everything by the book; no grounds for appeal because we overlooked something along the way. Look mate, I get how keen you are to see them, but there's still a member or two of Hickman's gang out there. We bring Kaden in too early and that gang member thinks he'll curry favour with his boss by getting rid of our star witness and *bam!* Our case expires like wet fireworks."

"I get that, Smithy, but I want some hope there's now an end in sight." Jack wandered out onto his veranda and looked towards O'Reilly's Ridge. A full moon was rising and the eastern face of the plug was almost luminous. His gaze tracked down and to the left, towards the spot where Anna's cottage lay dark and lonely. Empty like him until the moment the news story had given hope back.

"It will take time, but yes; at some point in the future, Anna and Kaden should be able to come home."

"Is there any chance I can talk to her before then?"

"Not even for you, mate. I won't compromise their safety."

"And I wouldn't expect you to. It's just—" He dragged in a steadying breath and rubbed a hand over that place in his chest that had ached from the moment on the ridge when the rope that linked them had fallen on his head. "Tell her for me."

"What shall I tell her, Jack?"

"Tell her I'll be here waiting for her. For them."

##

"Mrs Maloney, good morning." Jack kept his surprise at the sight of Freda Maloney under wraps. She was elderly, but there was nothing of the sweet granny he'd imagined about her. The woman holding the door had the deep wrinkles and leathery skin of someone who had spent most of their life out of doors. Eighty if she was a day, she wore faded jeans and a beige man's shirt with the sleeves rolled back, and a pair of boots coated in fresh dirt.

"I'm sorry to intrude on your work day. My name is Jack Donaldson. I phoned earlier about leasing the old church in town for a client."

From her five foot nothing height, Freda Maloney looked him up and down with the disdain of a queen. "You can come in, only because you're a sight for sore eyes. Whisky?"

Jack risked a glance at his watch. Nine-thirty in the morning. "Ah, not for me thanks. I have to see clients when I get back to the office. They might not take me seriously if they smell whisky on my breath."

"I guess I'll let you get away with that one. There are some prudes in town who don't think a woman my age should be drinking. Or still working with her cows either."

"What type of cattle do you have?"

"Jersey girls. Best milk for making cheese, and the best

cheeses you'll ever taste. Don't tell me you haven't tried my Whisky Flat cheeses?"

"That's *your* cheese? I didn't know. The blue cheese is brilliant."

"Thought you'd be a *blue* man. I can tell you've got good taste. Now, what is it you want to do with my building? You do know the church was deconsecrated forty or so years ago?"

"Yes, and that suits my client very well. She wants to open a gallery with arts and perhaps local craftwork. You might have heard of her–Anna Wilkins?"

"The woman with the deaf brother. I've heard of her. Painter, isn't she?" Freda poured a generous serve of whisky into a cut glass and drank.

"A very good painter. Landscapes, portraits—"

"And you like her and want to seal the deal for her. Got your eye on her, haven't you?"

"Mrs Maloney, I won't lie to you. I'm in love with her and when she eventually gets home to Lark Creek, I want to—"

"Bed her? Wed her?"

"Both, and probably in that order."

Freda tossed off the rest of her whisky and set the glass down. "I like you. Straight talker. Come back tomorrow evening with a contract. Leave the rent amount and length of contract spaces blank while I think about them and I'll fill in the details with you." She eyed him as she stood. "Maybe you can have that whisky with me then."

Jack stood and shook the hand she offered. "It would be a pleasure. Thanks."

Chapter 26

Anna picked up her most recent sketches and piled them on the kitchen bench as Smithy pulled out a chair and joined Kaden at the square dining table. Three months worth of her artwork lay scattered around the small lounge and stood in a stack of canvases below the breakfast counter.

Smithy drew the mug of coffee Anna had made towards him and drank before setting it down and meeting her gaze. "This is welcome after that long drive, thanks."

"You're welcome. We wondered how long it would be before we saw you again. I told Kaden you'd probably be caught up in preparation of the case against his uncle." Itching to know how it was progressing and when the trial would be, she'd lain awake many nights, scanning the internet for news, anything that might give her a clue to the date of their likely return home.

"You were right about that. We've pulled a lot of late nighters and a helluva lot of overtime, but we're just about ready for the first stage. And one more piece of good news; the police in Brisbane picked up the last couple of Hickman's gang in a raid last week.

"Listen Anna, I've got a proposition for you and Kaden to consider and I want you both to hear me out before you say anything. Will you translate that, and what I'm about to say?"

"Of course." She looked at Kaden and signed. *This sounds important.*

He signed back quickly, his eyes bright and hopeful. *Do you think we can go home?*

Anna's thoughts flew immediately to Lark Creek and Jack, but where did Kaden regard as home now his uncle was in jail awaiting trial?

Which home?

Our home, the cottage. Where else would I go? Unless—you don't want me? A sudden flush of heat rose in Kaden's cheeks and his gaze skittered away.

Anna's response was instinctive. *Of course I want you. Why wouldn't I want you?*

Jack. You want to be alone with Jack. He pushed up from the table and his chair crashed to the floor.

Moments later, Ted appeared at Anna's front door. "Everything okay in here?"

Smithy waved nonchalantly at the security man. "All fine. Teenage angst I'm guessing."

Ted nodded, replaced his gun in the back of his jeans and pulled his hoodie down over it before he closed the door behind him. Winter cold had followed him inside, and Kaden had stormed out the back door, leaving it wide open to the westerly wind. The chill in the small apartment was instant.

Smithy eyed her over his mug of coffee. "Not quite the reaction I expected to my introduction. What was that about?"

Anna rubbed her temples as a familiar tension headache returned. "Unresolved questions about Kaden's future. Jack and I skirted around the issue because it felt like it was so far in the future—we weren't sure if any of us even had a future before you caught Hickman. Kaden asked if we were going home. He caught me off guard when I asked which home he meant. When he said the cottage, I hesitated too long before I answered."

"And now he thinks you don't want him and he has nowhere to go?"

"Something like that. Only it's not true."

"That's why I'm here, to talk about going home, and what your options are. Let me get him back to the table and we'll start again." Smithy drank another mouthful of coffee before heading through the back door in pursuit of Kaden.

Anna sat, her mind whirling around possibilities, around the future Smithy had mentioned. It was hard to imagine they now had one. What would it look like? Was Jack still in Lark Creek after all this time? *Six months*, he'd said. Six months to get the solicitor's office running smoothly and he'd be heading back to Brisbane, to that partner's position he wanted. His six months would be up by now. If she could return to Lark Creek with Kaden, would Jack be there?

Kaden's mouth was turned down in a pout, but he came willingly enough with Smithy's arm over his shoulders. He looked from Smithy to Anna. *Sorry. What did he say?*

Anna explained there was a proposition they had to consider. *Mention of home caught me off guard, the idea of us going home after so long.*

He nodded and asked, *What's the proposition?*

Smithy faced Kaden while Anna translated. "Would you like to be assessed for top of the line, state of the art hearing aids?"

Kaden's eyes widened and the sulky teenager disappeared, replaced by an excited child looking at a longed-for gift. *Of course.*

"Would you consider boarding at a school for hearing-impaired students where you'll be able to learn to speak once the aids have been fitted?"

With Anna? Kaden looked from her to Smithy, waiting for an answer or a body cue.

What Smithy was suggesting was an option that would open the way for her to reunite with Jack but separate her from Kaden. For the first time since meeting him, Anna realised that Kaden had slipped under her skin, teenage traumas and all. They'd been through so much together and he'd come to rely on her as the only constant in his life. She cared for him and about him, and the idea of being separated touched her in a way she'd not expected when she'd agreed to take on his care and communication. "Kaden asked if I'd be there with him?"

"You could visit as often as you want to, but the school is

actually beside a Defence Force facility down in Canberra." Smithy didn't blink as he turned from Kaden and held her gaze, and Anna realised there was a subtext meant for her.

She replayed his last comment in her mind. The location was the key, but what did it mean to her? "How long would he be there?"

"Minimum time? Until Hickman's trial is over. But before you translate that, there's more. If he wishes, Kaden could be enrolled in a twelve-month introduction to the army course and begin university study in a course of his choosing. Graham Peyton offered to bring him up to speed in fitness and bushcraft skills."

"So he'd be spending some time with Graham first?"

"Yes. Way out bush, completely off the grid."

Anna nodded and explained the opportunity to Kaden. *What do you think? Do you need time to consider?*

What's the other choice?

Smithy looked down at his hands, tapping two fingers on the table before he looked at Kaden. "We move you and Anna to a new location every few weeks until your uncle's trial is over. You can stay together, but move often, or you can get fitted with hearing aids and go bush with Graham, and I do mean *bush*, until you're ready to take the entrance test for the army. Anna would not be with you once you had the hearing aids. The choice is yours to make."

Kaden shook his head. *Not my choice. Ours. Me and Anna.*

Smithy smiled and finished his coffee. "I'll leave you two to discuss your choices. I'm going downstairs for a chat. Come and tell me if you reach a decision before I go."

Kaden put out a hand to stop Smithy and asked one more question. *The hearing aids—can I get them whichever way I choose?*

"For sure, but I'm guessing learning to speak might be easier if you live in at the school for a while. Which means a bit of time away from Anna."

Once Smithy had gone, they sat quietly, with occasional glances at each other. The choice was clear to her, but Kaden needed to arrive at the conclusion for himself.

At last he met her eyes. *What do you think?*

The first way, we stay together, I keep helping you, but we move often. The second way, we are apart for a while but you learn how to help yourself. Then you can come home to me if you like. I'll accept your choice. Which one is right for you?

I don't want to leave you, but I want to hear and to speak for myself.

Anna knew the strength of that desire to be independent. She'd seen it in the way her parents lived their lives, and in the choices they'd made when they discovered they had a child who could hear.

The army offer would let you study at university if you wanted to. It could set you up with a job and give you independence.

Kaden nodded slowly. *Would I have to choose my course now or could I think about it for a while?*

I imagine you could decide later. Was he tipping towards the choice Anna was confident would be the making of him, the choice that would give him freedom and a guaranteed future?

The choice that gave her a chance to find Jack.

And if she found him?

Would things be the same as before?

Chapter 27

Small town lawyer, she'd called him. Jack hadn't corrected her. If this was where Anna wanted to be, he would remain in Lark Creek and make it true. The allure of working fifteen-hour days if he wanted to make partner had waned the longer he stayed in Lark Creek. It wasn't that he was lazy; nobody could accuse him of that. But there was so much more to life out of the big city.

There was Anna . . .

Or there could be. According to Smithy, Kaden had chosen to go to a school for hearing-impaired students in Canberra. Anna had accompanied him to see him settled in and be with him while he was fitted with hearing aids. The prohibition on contact was still in place, but Smithy had promised him it wouldn't be for long.

Gazing through the front window of Anna's cottage at bare branches whipping in the winter wind, Jack drank his beer. Hours of cleaning up after the forensic team had finished had led to him staying over. Since then he'd spent every weekend out here. Sleeping in Anna's bed with the faintest hint of her scent in her pillow, he hoped for that miracle Smithy had promised.

Picking up a work file, he set his beer on the side table and dropped onto the couch that had been his bed in the early days of their charade. He much preferred to sit than sleep on it. Flicking over a few pages seeking a particular clause he needed to redraft, the flashing blue light of Graham's silent alarm took him by surprise. He jumped up and raced into the bedroom. The monitors were still connected to the cameras. He hadn't thought to disconnect them in the months since that daring night escape over the ridge.

Heart thudding madly, he scanned the images. The camera

at the front gate revealed nothing more than a set of bright headlights at the wrong angle to see who his visitor was. He adjusted the camera angle and zoomed in as much as he was able to, in time to see the back of a man's head climbing into the driver's seat before the door closed and the driver drove through, leaving the gate open.

For a quick getaway?

Jack bolted through the back door and past the garden shed just in time. He slid to a halt behind the wood pile and watched as the vehicle eased around behind the cottage. The black four-wheel drive was covered in dust and mud splashes and looked as though it had driven some distance.

From Brisbane? There'd been rain to the east of town earlier in the day.

The vehicle turned and pulled up near the back steps, facing back down the driveway before the engine was turned off.

Jack edged backwards, eyes on the vehicle as he felt for the corner of the wood pile. The driver's door opened and a shadowy figure climbed out. A familiar movement brought bile rushing into Jack's throat. A moment later, light from the kitchen confirmed it. Now he could see a handgun held steadily between both hands.

The passenger door opened and a figure stepped out.

"Anna, stay in the car."

Anna? And the voice was Smithy's.

Jack froze for a heartbeat—two beats. "Anna!" Conscious of Smithy's drawn gun, he left the shelter of the wood pile, hands extended either side. "Don't shoot, Smithy. It's Jack."

"Jack!" The passenger door flew open and Anna ran to him and flung her arms around his neck.

His arms closed around Anna, holding her close, holding her like he'd never let her go. Burying his face in her hair, he breathed in her scent. Beneath his hands he could feel her bones too easily. "Let me look at you."

"I'd rather kiss you."

Smithy strolled over, the click as he flicked on the safety of his gun audible in a lull in the wind. "Save it, kids, and come in out of the cold. God, it's freezing out here. Give me the coast any day. Jack, how are you?"

Unwilling to let Anna go, Jack compromised by tucking her against his side and extending his right hand. "Now—I'm fine, but you could have texted you were coming, mate. Five minutes ago I was shitting myself thinking you were more of Hickman's boys."

Anna wrapped both arms around his waist and rested her head on his shoulder. "That's my fault. I wanted to surprise you. We showed up at your house in town and when we saw it was in darkness, Smithy guessed you'd be out here. Forgive me?"

"I forgive you, but I may need lots of TLC to soothe my shattered nerves."

Smithy pretended to put a finger down his throat. "Please, folks, can you keep it PG-rated until I've gone? Some of us don't want to hear about your love life."

They strolled back to the house and into the kitchen. Jack settled Anna on his lap. He had no intention of letting her go, regardless of Smithy's sensitivities. "You don't want to hear because you don't have a love life of your own."

"I don't want one, that's the difference. Okay, I'm putting the kettle on and having a coffee and then I'm heading into town, finding a nice little hotel and sleeping for the next twelve hours straight."

Anna shook her head. "We have a spare room—"

Smithy raised a hand and shook his head. "Thanks Anna, but I won't crash your reunion party. You two have waited far too long for tonight. But I'll take any recommendations for accommodation."

Anna glanced at her watch. "Ring Katy Leonard. It's not too late and she may have a room at her B and B. Failing that, the hotel on Main Street has a few rooms, but it might be noisy on a Friday night."

"Thanks, I'll call now while the kettle's boiling." Smithy disappeared into the lounge. A moment later, his call must have been answered and the low tones of enquiry filtered through the open doorway.

Anna took Jack's face between her hands and gazed into his eyes. Her soft brown gaze ran over his face and her fingers slipped into his longer hair. "About that kiss—"

He needed no second invitation. "Long overdue." Their mouths found each other with a hunger that not even Smithy's return interrupted. The kettle whistled and stopped before the back door gently closed.

Some time later—minutes or hours, Jack wasn't certain and cared even less—he lifted his head and rested his forehead against Anna's. "I think it's past our bedtime."

"Way past."

He rose with Anna in his arms and carried her down the hall to her room—their room.

As he set her down on the bed and lay beside her, she looked up, a shy smile on her face. "I wasn't sure you'd still be in Lark Creek when I got back. I thought you might have gone back to Brisbane and taken up that partnership."

He leaned up on his elbow and tucked a strand of hair behind her ear. "Didn't Smithy pass on my message?"

"He said you told him you'd be here, but it's been so long I thought—I didn't know if you'd wait for me." Her shy uncertainty almost undid him. Didn't she have any idea of the hold she had of his heart?

"Anna, I'd wait for you forever if need be. When that rope fell on me up on the ridge that night, keeping you safe was the only thing on my mind. But afterwards, I regretted not telling you how much I love you. That should have been the last thing you heard me say. I want it to be the last thing you hear every night from now on."

"I'd like that too."

"So Anna, I love—"

Her finger stopped his lips completing the declaration and he frowned. "What's wrong?"

"Before we reach *the last thing*, we need to talk about Kaden and what's going to happen with him."

Jack wrapped his hand around hers and kissed the tips of each finger. "My darling, I'll talk all you want about Kaden in the morning, but there isn't anything we can do about him tonight. There is, however, another man here who's dying for your touch and who wants to make love to you. Right. Now."

"In that case . . . I love you, Jack."

"I love you, Anna. Always."

Epilogue

"Quick, Jack, Kaden's bus is coming down the road." Anna pushed a loose strand of hair behind her ear, all but bouncing on her toes. The summer heat was building, but in the shade of a stand of eucalyptus trees, it was bearable.

Jack locked the car, raced over and slung an arm over her shoulders as they waited at Lark Creek's new bus stop across the road from the police station. "There's quite a turn out to meet the first bus to make the Lark Creek run."

"Half the town seems to be here. There's Graham and— Jack? Graham's holding Janice Lehman's hand. You didn't tell me about them."

Jack glanced across and waved to Graham, who sketched a wave back. "Thought you knew. Guess you've been so involved setting up your gallery, you didn't notice."

"How could you not tell me something as important as that? We'll have to invite Janice to Kaden's welcome home barbecue too."

"Great idea."

With a hissing of brakes, the bus pulled up and the door swung open. First off was a young, dark-haired woman. Rhoda and Leon Alexopoulos rushed over to her and enveloped her in a group hug.

"That's their niece, Nefeli, come to Australia from Greece for an extended visit." Jack seemed to know all the local gossip these days, and Anna wondered if just maybe she'd been a little too focused on setting up the gallery.

Two more locals descended from the bus and then Kaden appeared. Anna's heart leapt with pride, as though he really was her little brother come home for a visit. Tears pricked her eyes and she sniffed before holding her arms out to him. Kaden walked over, leaned down and hugged her.

"You've grown since you left home. And gosh, you look smart in your uniform."

"Thank you."

At the sound of his voice, Anna's tears spilled over. She waved her hands in front of her face. "Don't mind me. I'm just being silly."

Graham and Janice joined them and Graham shook Kaden's hand. "Welcome home, mate."

"It's great to be home for Christmas. Hello Janice. Nice to see you."

Janice put a hand on Kaden's arm and kissed his cheek. "Wait till you hear our news. It's all happening and it's thanks to you."

Anna shook her head. "Now I really feel out of it. What have I missed?"

Jack took her hand and kissed the back of it. "Told you, you need to poke your nose out of the gallery every so often."

"Graham and I are starting up an outdoor activities school for students with disabilities. The paperwork and permissions have taken ages, but it's thanks to this young man that it's happening at all."

"How wonderful! We'd love to hear more about it. Would you like to come to a barbecue at our place, five o'clock if you can make it."

Graham grinned. He was smiling more than Anna had ever seen him and even seemed relaxed in the crowd at the bus stop. She was happy for him, and glad he was apparently taking a chance on love again.

Jack pointed at a khaki duffel bag as the driver hauled it out from storage. "Looks like that's yours, Kaden."

Kaden glanced at the bus. "I'll get it. Then can we go

home?"

"Of course, mate."

Graham and Janice left with a promise to attend the barbecue. "We'll bring wine and beer," Janice said before they turned back towards her car.

"Jack, is it just me or is there something special about Cottage Farm?"

"It's cute and cosy, but it's the people who make a place special. The cottage is our home as much as it's Kaden's. We might not be related by blood, but we are a family and tonight, we're going to celebrate being home—together."

THE END

Want to know when Susanne Bellamy's next books will be released?
Follow her on:

Bookbub: https://www.bookbub.com/authors/susanne-bellamy
OR
On Facebook: https://www.facebook.com/susannebellamyauthor/

About the Author

I love travel—new places, new faces, different cultures and endless possibilities. I've cruised from Australia to Britain and back through the Suez Canal when I was a child, trekked in Nepal and Vietnam, lived briefly in Noumea, visited western Europe and west coast America among other places. Let me repeat—I love travel! And history.

People's stories fascinate me. Past and present lives and relationships and the mysterious ways Fate works. Even how I met my husband—Fate. Wonderful and mysterious.

And so my stories explore the wonderful and mysterious ways in which people meet. I should probably thank the flat-mate who locked me out of my new house years ago, which led directly to meeting my husband. But that's another story!

I am a member of the Romance Writers of Australia and love to hear from fellow romance authors and readers alike.

Read more at: http://www.susannebellamy.com/

Other Books

Visit Susanne's website to see more books:

http://www.susannebellamy.com/books-by-susanne-bellamy.html

Or on my website: http://www.susannebellamy.com

Read on for a sneak peek at
'In the Heat of the Night' *(Bindarra Creek: A Town Reborn), coming this August 2019.*

Chapter 1

The Cyprus Café lunch crowd was thinning as Thalia Levonis took the tray of *baklava* from the display cabinet and picked up a pair of tongs. "How many pieces would you like, Mrs Ainslie?"

Esther Ainslie pulled a piece of paper from her handbag and consulted it before she settled on, "Seven, no, better make it eight please, Thalia. Ty Devereaux is joining us tonight."

"Annie's fiancé? Wow, does he know he's coming into a book club with all women members?"

"I'm pleased to say he knows and is looking forward to a lively discussion. His presence means we're now a mixed club. Maybe we'll be able to encourage a few more males to join now he's leading the charge." She folded her list and slipped it back into her handbag. "I wonder if I should get something else for nibbles? Men usually like to eat more than we women. Give me a minute to have another think, dear."

"No problem, Mrs Ainslie." Thalia closed the cabinet door and turned to the next customer. The dark blue eyes of Bindarra Creek's fire brigade captain sent tremors fluttering in her stomach before reality crashed around her. Once upon a time she had thought she could be the woman who won his sole attention. *About ten women ago.*

"Kel, what can I do for you?"

"Ah, Thali, that's a loaded question for a beautiful woman to ask a man." He gave her the same smile he offered every female in Bindarra Creek, whether they were eight or eighty. And every one of them probably reacted the same way she did, felt the same stirring in the belly, like the heartburn of indigestion only not so easy to get over. It didn't help that she secretly liked the way he shortened her name. It rolled off his tongue like he thought it was an endearment. And that was absolutely not okay.

"My name is Tha-li-a. Three syllables with an a on the end." She'd long ago given up on what Mama called *catching his eye*, and now, she wasn't even certain she liked him. Kel wasn't exactly a womaniser. He treated the women he went out with well, but no one woman had ever held his attention for long.

She tipped her head to the side and tried to remember this was Mama and Papa's café. Telling a customer what she longed to say wouldn't be good for business. "Let me rephrase that. What would you like—from the cabinet or the menu?"

"Spoilsport." He winked and turned his gaze to the blackboard above her head. "Something hot I think, with a touch of spicy heat." His gaze flicked to Thalia.

He thinks he can charm me with that old cliché, he's got another think coming.

She pressed her lips together. No, she didn't like him, or the way her body angled towards him, responding of its own accord. She moved away and leaned on the counter, pressing her hands down hard to remind herself not to give him the satisfaction of showing any interest in him.

Thalia waited for Esther Ainslie to decide, hoping she took all the time in the world to make her selection. Maybe Mama would return from the kitchen and deal with Captain *I'm-so-wonderful* Jones before she had to attend to him again.

The retired librarian was watching her with a curious expression. She nodded once, as though filing something in her memory.

Shoot, had she been so preoccupied thinking about Kel, she'd missed hearing Esther's order?

"So, Mrs Ainslie, what looks good to you?"

"I think I'll take some of those *spanakopites* too please, dear. Seeing we now have men attending our book club."

Kel leaned on the counter and turned his blue-eyed charm on Esther. "Mrs Ainslie, never tell me you've opened up the ladies book club of Bindarra Creek to we poor intellectually-starved men?"

"Wouldn't hurt you to come along, Kel. Some lively discussion of great books and stories to touch your heart."

"Fifty Shades, no thanks. I'm not into that stuff."

Thalia set Esther's box of *spanakopites* on top of the glass cabinet. "How do you know what *stuff* is in those books if you've never read them?"

Kel's mouth opened and closed, like the fish her brother Nico had caught when he was ten-years-old. The one that fell off the hook and, with an indignant flick of its tail, disappeared in the swift-flowing waters of the Akuna River.

"Got me there, Thali—sorry, Tha-li-a. It's just what I've heard from some of BC's ladies."

Now, his use of the diminutive of her name grated, and his attempt at humour . . .

What did I ever see in this arrogant man?

She folded her arms and pinned him with a look that could have come straight from Medusa. Good Greek girl that she was, she knew Kel wasn't the marrying kind.

"Well in *our* book club, we read good books in all sorts of genres. Everyone takes a turn to choose a book for the year and each month we meet in the home of one of our members. Tonight, is Mrs Ainslie's turn to host."

"Our—you're in this book club too, are you?"

"Of course. It's my turn next month to host." Thalia gently

packed Esther's purchases in her reusable shopping bag, refusing to let Kel's needling affect the care she gave to the task.

Kel leaned on the glass cabinet and watched her with a searching look and a grin that would melt Esther's *baklava* if it got in the way. "And what book have you chosen, Thalia? A modern Greek tragedy?"

"I did consider *Fire on the Water*, but I've always wanted to see the Silk Road, so that's what mine is about. It's written from a travel writer's perspective."

That caught his attention. Not that Thalia was trying to. No, that hope was more shrivelled than crumbs in the toaster. But stirring Kel? That was always on the cards. "One day I'm going to travel along parts of that route."

"With a tour group?"

She was well aware that Kel's preferred style of travel was solo.

What was it he'd said on his return from his last trip to Nepal? *Only tourists travel in groups. Real travellers immerse themselves in their surroundings and don't whinge when there's no fresh orange juice for breakfast.*

Kel didn't think much of people who went to overseas countries and then complained that it wasn't like home. No groups would hold back the captain of Bindarra Creek Fire and Rescue when he set off on his annual adventure holiday.

"I prefer not to be locked into a group when I travel. I like exploring by myself, and besides, I enjoy walking. I want my feet to touch the ground where caravans passed carrying all sorts of exotic goods to the ends of the known world. And I'll stay in *caravanserai*. I imagine those inns still exist in some form along the route."

Kel's gaze narrowed and fixed on her until a rush of embarrassed heat raced up her cheeks. Most times she kept her passion and dreams of travel under wraps, but Kel Jones brought out her fire.

"If you're going to walk the Silk Road you're going to have to be really fit, Thali. It's not for the faint-hearted, but frankly, I wouldn't recommend it to a lone woman traveller. Not in some of the places the road passes through."

Her chin rose and she looked down her nose at him, as much as a five foot three woman could to a man who was at least six feet tall. "Because we're the weaker sex? How outdated that attitude is. Why, if I—"

Kel raised a hand to stem her tirade. "Thalia, I don't consider women weak. Far from it. We have lots of women in both the rural fire brigades and the Fire and Rescue teams and they're wonderful at their jobs. But on the Silk Road—there are areas where a lone woman would be seen as fair game."

She put her hands on her hips and glared. Of course, he was right, but the fact it was Kel telling her what to do rankled. Bravado had always been her defence around him—*current glare included.* "Do you think I haven't thought long and hard about the dangers of such a trip?"

"I'm sure you've researched what to expect, but culturally, it's a difficult area for women travelling on their own."

She huffed and looked down at the tongs she hadn't realised she'd picked up again. Setting them in their container, she closed the cabinet door. "Right, okay—so it's dangerous. I do understand that. I'm not ignorant of the situation in those countries."

"Not just dangerous—it would be a really bad decision. But Thali, I don't doubt that you could walk the whole of the Silk Road if you decided to."

Was that meant to mollify her? He didn't look like he was trying to be smart with her. In fact, he looked genuinely concerned that she might really intend to walk the road alone. His concern took her by surprise. Was it possible that Kel Jones cared about her, even the tiniest little bit? The idea was bittersweet now she'd given up the idea of ever catching his eye. "So long as we're clear about that.”

Esther moved back into their conversation, recalling Thalia to the fact the former librarian had a prior claim on being served. With an effort, she replaced her glare with a customer-friendly smile. “Was there anything else, Mrs Ainslie?”

“Yes, you can stop calling me Mrs Ainslie now you’re twenty-eight. I know good manners were drilled into you by your parents, but we’re both adults and in the book club together. You don’t call me missus there so please don’t use it here. We’re friends, Thalia, first and foremost, we’re friends.” She turned to Kel with a guileless smile that didn’t fool Thalia.

She knew Esther’s mild manner hid a backbone of steel. Whatever she’d decided was going to happen, would.

“Kel, why don’t you come along and join us this evening? You and Ty can band together and give us a male perspective on—”

Both Kel’s hands rose, warding off danger. “Whoa, Esther, much as I’d love to join you, I’m not—”

“Stop right there, Kel. I know you enjoy reading. Penny happened to share that information when I went in to pick up my copy of Thalia’s choice of book for next month. Adventure stories and biographies of famous explorers are top of your purchases.”

Kel shook his head. “It’s a sad day when a man can’t trust his bookshop owner to keep his secrets. I’ll have a word to say next time I’m in Penny Lane Book Shop.”

Esther drew her handbag into the crook of her arm and held it close. “I suggest you ask her for a copy of that book about the Silk Road and come and join us next month. With your travels in Nepal I’m sure you could offer a unique perspective.”

“I’m sure I could. Tell you what, Esther, the day Thalia joins the fire service is the day I’ll come to your book club.”

Thalia’s BS radar pinged long and loud. *How dare Kel make fun of the group of women who met once a month to share their love of books? How dare he?* She drew herself up until she was all but on tiptoes, rested both hands on the counter and leaned towards him. "Is that so?" Did the man really expect her not to rise to the challenge? Thalia pinned him with a direct look he had no chance of escaping. "Where do I sign up?"

Kel grinned like a Cheshire Cat; like he thought she was being cute. *The arrogant vlaka didn't believe her.*

Fury beyond any Greek drama surged through Thalia. She was past caring that customers at the nearest tables were casting amused looks their way or craning their necks to see what had stirred the usually placid eldest daughter of Thea and Stavros Levonis. She would prick Kel's arrogant, egotistical, *thinks-he's-superior* bubble and show him.

She opened her mouth to tell Kel precisely what she thought of his attitude.

His pager went off.

Everyone knew what that meant—a fire or accident requiring his crew.

He looked at the screen before he met Thalia's gaze. "Call out—I've got to go. Come and see me at the station later today if you're serious. If not—" He turned to Esther. "Enjoy your book discussion tonight." With no time to wait for food, Kel headed for the door.

"He has no intention of coming along, unless you were serious about signing up?" Esther paused, the fifty-dollar note halfway out of her purse and settled a needle-sharp gaze on Thalia. "Were you?"

Thalia looked at the door Kel had exited through, as though he might be there listening for her answer, certain it had been nothing more than a throwaway line. "Maybe I will check it out, even if all I do is give Captain Jones a surprise. I like the idea of putting him off balance."

"Good for you, Thalia. And you can bring him along tonight after you've signed up."

***

The alarm woop-wooped at Bindarra Creek Fire Station. Kel gulped down the half mug of coffee he'd grabbed while waiting for his crew to assemble, glad he'd only gone as far as the Cyprus Café for lunch. If only he'd managed to grab a bite instead of stirring Thali, although it had been fun. He enjoyed provoking her until her eyes flashed and veiled insults dropped from her mouth.

The scrape of heavy boots on concrete alerted him to the arrival of some of his team. Connor Jacobs rocked in behind Lou Baker and Gabe, completing the crew needed to take the appliance out.

Kel took out his jacket, helmet, and two-way radio from the locker, picked up the co-ordinates of the fire and joined the crew on the truck. Mandy Kaminsky raced into the station. Their newest recruit was breathing hard and pink-cheeked. Kel stopped, door handle in his grip. "It's fine, Mandy. We've got a team, but you can look after the comms and start on the report now you're here."

She waved a hand in acknowledgement and sucked in a deep breath. "Sorry, I ran all the way from the shop. I'm not as fit as I thought."

"Worth focusing on next training day." Kel slid into his seat on the passenger side and looked across at Connor. "Everybody right to go?"

A chorus of checks greeted him. "Good. Head east on Mt Ingalls Road." He entered the details on the touch screen.

Mandy stepped into the road and checked before giving them the all-clear. Kel switched on the siren and lights before Connor exited the station and turned right along the main east-west street.

Connor glanced at the screen. "Looks like the fire is near Angus McGregor's place." Connor eased back at the intersection with Main Street. Mid-morning traffic stopped for the fire engine to pass. Once through the crossroads, he increased speed and the truck headed out of town.

Kel nodded and read the sparse information on the print out again. "Yeah, the rural crew at Glenmeer are already attending a grass fire the other side of their area so we picked up the call."

"Not what I expected at the end of winter." Connor passed the eighty-kilometre road sign and increased speed.

"There's a lot of pockets of long dry grass, despite that rain and the local flooding last month." Kel's phone rang. He pulled it from his pocket, looked at the screen and accepted the call. "Angus, we're on our way, about five minutes from you now. How's it looking out there?" A plume of white smoke rose above the trees with a slight angle to the west. When the truck topped a rise in the road, Kel tried to estimate the size of the fire. *Not big yet.*

"Not so close that the house is in danger, but the wind has started to pick up and it's turning the fire towards us."

"Is your exit in danger?"

"No, we're fine, but I've got Claire and Ollie to pack a bag just in case. Meg is sleeping. Look, I'll meet you at the entrance and bring you in. It will be quicker if I show you the way. The fire front is close to the dam if you want to pump from that."

"Will do, thanks. See you in a few minutes." He turned to his crew. "We'll be drafting from one of Angus' dams so get the suction hose out."

Lou sketched a corny salute. "Sure thing, Captain."

Kel grinned. "Lou Baker, when did you start getting so formal?"

Angus McGregor was standing beside his ute at the entrance to Craigellachie, his family property. As the appliance turned onto his driveway, Angus got into the ute and led the way through gates he'd opened before the fire fighters arrived. The appliance pulled up behind the ute and stopped beside the dam. The fire was low and lacking fuel now the wind had turned it back on scorched ground.

Kel joined Angus while the crew unrolled the suction hose

and set up. "Thanks, Angus. We'll take it from here. Claire and the children will be happier if you go back to them. I know she must be anxious."

"Mate, anxious doesn't begin to cover it. She's over dealing with fires."

"Fact of life in this part of the world, but we've got this. Tell her she'll be able to sit down tonight and have a family dinner in her own home."

Angus nodded. Kel's reassurance eased the worried frown that had marred his friend's face since the crew arrived. "Thanks. That's a relief." He turned the ute in a wide half circle around the appliance and headed back through the gate. Back to his family and his home.

Having a wife and children to worry about would be hell. Glad that he'd avoided that stress, Kel focused on the task at hand.